HEALING HO[

Club Isola 2

Avery Gale

MENAGE AMOUR

Siren Publishing, Inc.
www.SirenPublishing.com

HEALING HOLLY

Club Isola 2

AVERY GALE
Copyright © 2014

Chapter 1

Gage Hughes had worked for two years on the small island off the Virginia coast that was the location of one of the east coast's most exclusive BDM clubs. The years he'd spent working as a Special Forces operative had been exhilarating—hell, it had basically been a five-year adrenaline rush. But he'd opted out and found he was enjoying the slower pace that working security offered. Tonight he'd looked on as his friend and boss, club owner Ian McGregor had married Callie Reece in a sunset ceremony on the beach below his home. Now the newlyweds, along with their third, Jace Garrett were on Club Isola's small stage in the main lounge.

The room was filled to capacity with the large crowd of invited guests. Only a select few knew that Ian and Callie had already gotten married, so his boss's announcement had brought loud cheers from everyone in attendance. Everyone who met Ian's new wife was taken in by her. From what Gage had seen the tiny blonde was smart as a whip, had a killer sense of humor, was completely clueless about how beautiful she was, and had a submissive streak a mile wide. That wasn't to say that she hadn't challenged Ian and Jace, but Ian's devotion to Callie was obvious to everyone who saw them together.

Living so far from his own family, Gage had quickly come to appreciate the family-like atmosphere of the McGregor Holdings security team. Gage had grown up on a large Texas ranch next door to the one operated by Jace Garrett's family. Both families had kept on working when it would have been easy to sit back and live off their oil income. But Gage and Jace's fathers had steadfastly maintained that working hard kept them young and their children out of trouble, so they had kept the ranches active and growing.

Leaning back against the wall, Gage watched the crowd with an avid intensity. After a breach of security traumatized Callie and led to her being injured, none of McGregor Holdings' security staff was taking any chances. Callie wasn't just the boss's wife, she'd managed to endear herself to each and every member of the small island's residents. Gage knew that Ian had hired Jace as his corporate Chief of Security as soon as he'd heard Jace planned to retire from the SEALS. Jace had met Ian in college and they'd become fast friends. They had stayed in touch after graduation when Ian had returned to Washington D.C. to take over his father's faltering business after the man had died suddenly. Jace had joined the navy and quickly moved on to the SEAL teams.

One night after a serious round of drinking, Jace had told Gage that Ian had gone *above and beyond* to maintain contact after they had graduated. Jace's respect for Ian McGregor was obvious when he'd explained that even as Ian was up to his ass in alligators trying to save the struggling business his father had nearly bankrupted, he'd kept in regular contact. Jace had laughed that his own parents hadn't even attended his SEAL graduation because it had been branding season, but Ian had flown clear across the country to attend the ceremony and reception. As a former Army Ranger, Gage understood exactly how important graduations from Special Forces trainings were—hell his own family had opted to stay in Europe on vacation rather than attend his ceremony. Gage's family worked together, but they'd always valued money over people, and as a result, Gage tried to avoid trips back to Texas whenever he could. Jace on the other hand loved returning to his Texas roots—at least he did whenever he was willing to take the time off.

Listening to Ian's short announcement to those gathered together for Callie's collaring ceremony, Gage couldn't help the longing that washed through him. He wished he could find a woman that would be his other half, as Ian had just described Callie. Once he'd discovered the Ds lifestyle and the pleasure two men could bring a woman there had been no turning back, and from that time on Jace had known that he would likely end up in a polyamorous relationship. Before his friend and boss, Jace Garrett, had become Ian and Callie's permanent third, he and Gage had shared women in various scenes both in and outside of Club Isola. As a result, they'd discovered they had an almost telepathic connection, and besides the fact they worked well together, they had become extremely good friends as well.

Scanning the room once more, he noticed the petite, but curvy brunette standing at the back of the room just a short distance to his left. He remembered meeting her at the hospital after Callie had been attacked by Senator Westmore's crazy-assed wife, Nanette. Gage had been introduced to Holly Mills by Daphne Craig, Ian's right-hand executive assistant. He had been impressed that she kept up with Daphne, who had been known to work circles around all the former soldiers Ian employed. Keeping up with the elderly woman was no small feat in anyone's opinion. Hell, Gage didn't know a single one of Ian's employees that wasn't in awe of his feisty, but brilliant executive assistant.

Gage hadn't seen Holly Mills since that day, but she wasn't a woman any man was likely to forget. The tiny buxom beauty had luscious curves that made his hands itch to explore her softness. Her long, wavy brunette hair gleamed in the soft glow of the candlelight. The golden light was setting off the various shades of her hair making it look like it was almost sparkling. But the thing he remembered the most vividly was her bright green eyes, and Gage couldn't help wondering what color they would turn with her arousal. Would they become emerald or citron? Would they be laced with longing or heat?

Just as he was preparing to make another perimeter check he noticed one of the club subs making his way toward where Gage was standing. Since this was the sub who had been tasked with assisting at the stage tonight, Gage waited to find out what he needed. When the man stood in front of Gage, he bowed his head as a show of respect and then spoke quietly, "Master Gage, Master Jace asked that you secure the young woman at the back of the room. He said you'd know who he meant." Gage watched as the young man's eyes slid to Holly before returning to the floor. Gage tried to ignore the small curve he saw at the corners of the submissive's lips. He knew Reggie was a trusted regular at the club so he thanked him and sent him back to the stage. Gage made a mental note to arrange a scene on the St. Andrew's cross for the helpful sub the following night. He knew that despite the fact he was an up-and-coming congressman, the guy was a major pain slut.

Moving toward Holly, Gage took in the woman's body language at a glance. As an experienced Dom, reading every nuance of a woman's posture, stance, gestures, and expression was second nature. He remembered one night last summer when he and several of the Doms from the club had sat out on the beach drinking beer and discussing which training was more effective in teaching a man how to read a woman—Special Forces or Dom training. After a lengthy debate they had finally agreed to disagree since there was no clear-cut answer.

Gage walked up alongside Holly and immediately noted that she was so absorbed in what was happening on the stage that she wasn't even aware he'd come close enough to touch her. Teaching her to be more aware of her surroundings for her own safety should be a priority for her Dom—something he intended to mention to whoever claimed her. Suddenly it occurred to him that he'd only seen her on the island a few times and he'd never seen her inside the club. *Hmm, now isn't that interesting. Here she stands, obviously fascinated with the scene. Everything about her is proclaiming her arousal and she works for a man who owns a BDSM club. Wonder if she's a closet sub?*

Good God the woman was just "a little bit of a thing" as his daddy would say. She couldn't be more than five and a half feet tall and that was counting the killer heels she was currently wearing. At six and a half feet tall he still towered over her even with those stilts she probably called stilettos. He chuckled, thinking about how easily she'd fit between him and Jace because they were the same height. They'd have to be careful not to hurt her, hell they might lose her she was so tiny. But damn if the thought of her pressed between the two of them wasn't sending most of his blood double-timing it south of his belt in a very big way.

Gage watched the rapid rise and fall of her chest and knew the little doll was getting ready to orgasm just from watching the single-tail fall over the tanned skin of Callie's bare back. Gage could tell the men were pulling the lashes and he was sure he knew why. Ian wouldn't want Callie to have bad memories of her first night as his wife, yet he had also wanted to fulfill Club Isola's requirements for a club-hosted collaring ceremony as well. Gage knew it had been a tight-rope walk for Ian, and he had to give the man credit for ingenuity because he'd managed to pull both of his lashes and there were probably only a handful of people in the room who would have noticed.

Returning his attention to Holly, he stepped behind her and wrapped one arm around her so that it was just under her ample breasts. His move lifted her breasts so they reminded him of a lush offering. This position also made it easy for him to speak to her so that no one else could hear and to monitor her reactions to him.

Christ, the woman was almost ready to come, Gage could smell her arousal and would have loved to slide his hand up the inside of one of her thighs and play with her labia until it was swollen with need and then finger fuck her until she screamed his name. *Fuck, just touching her is frying my brain. Pay attention, Hughes.* With his forearm firmly encircling her he felt her jump and knew he had startled her. He leaned down and spoke in a hushed tone letting his lips barely brush the shell of her ear. "Are you enjoying the scene, beautiful girl?"

Gage was pleased when she settled back against his chest immediately and nodded. "Do you wish it was you tied to that cross? Do you wonder what pleasure that whip brings as it dances over Callie's delicate back warming her delicate skin in narrow lines placed in perfect symmetry by her Doms?" He felt her heart pounding against the walls of her chest and the panting of her respiration was becoming increasingly rapid and shallow as she moved quickly back toward the climax she'd been so close to before he'd distracted her. "Are you here because you work for Master Ian or because there is a part of you that feels like you are missing something?" He had deliberately referred to Ian by his Dom title rather than simply by his first name because it was important that she understood he was addressing the *submissive Holly* rather than the super-efficient employee he knew she had to be in order to survive working in Ian's executive offices.

He'd already noticed how her nipples were peaked and showing nicely through the shiny green silk of her halter dress. When she didn't answer either of his questions, he moved his hand to the tight peak of her left nipple and pinched it firmly between his thumb and index finger as he rasped against her ear, "Answer my question, Holly. Are you curious about the pleasures to be found in submission?"

Her breathless, "Yes," would have been sweet music to any Dom's ears.

Gage knew the scene was essentially over but he planned to get her as close to release as possible before Jace made his way up to where they were standing. "Close your eyes and focus on listening to my words, Holly." Watching as her long lashes drifted closed fanning over her porcelain cheeks, he used his free hand to signal Jace to come quickly and approach silently. One of the advantages of working with fellow former Special Forces operatives was that it was easy to use the hand signs they'd all had drilled into them. Those signals being second nature was often the narrow margin between a soldier's life and death. Gage smiled at Jace's raised eyebrow when he took in the way Holly's generous breasts were lifted in offering as Gage continued to roll her tight nipple firmly between his fingers.

"Remember—don't open your eyes until I tell you to." Gage knew by the tensing of her body when she felt Jace step up in front of her. "You felt Master Jace's presence, didn't you, sweetness? He's standing right in front of you and he's going to be speaking to you. He won't touch you for reasons he'll explain later, but you will answer his questions immediately and honestly, do you understand? And sweetheart, the only acceptable answer is 'Yes, sir.'"

Her answer was barely audible, but her quiet, breathless, "Yes, sir, I understand," was sweet indeed.

Chapter 2

Walking toward where Gage stood with the woman he'd asked his friend to secure, Jace nearly laughed out loud at Gage's very interesting definition of "secure." Gage's arm was wrapped around Holly's chest lifting her full breasts to the point they were practically ready to pop out of her silky halter top. She was already panting with need, her nipples were taut and peaked as if they were calling for his attention.

Listening as Gage let her know he wouldn't be touching her, Jace moved close enough that he was sure she'd be able to feel his body's heat move over her skin. Hearing her small gasp was a turn-on that made him long to slide his fingers under that pretty dress and help her climb up the mountain of release he knew she was chasing. But Gage had been right, he couldn't touch her yet, but that didn't stop him from looking his fill and it damn sure didn't stop the sweet scent of her arousal from wafting up to tease his nose before settling over his senses like a misty morning fog on his parents' ranch.

Gage knew he wouldn't touch her—at least not until he'd officially ended his time as Ian and Callie's *third* because a promise of fidelity was one he honored—always. But once that commitment was ended, all bets were off with the brunette beauty standing before him. Hell, he'd been fighting his attraction to her from the first moment he'd seen her. And tonight, seeing her reaction to Callie's collaring was enough to convince him that Holly Mills was indeed every bit as submissive as he'd thought she would be.

When he'd first noticed her standing at the back of the room, he'd been worried about how she would react to the single-tail whip both he and Ian planned to use. They had definitely pulled the lashes, but most people in the room wouldn't have known that and he was certain Holly wasn't experienced enough to have been able to see the difference. He'd finally resigned himself to the fact that it was probably good to find out up front how she would honestly react. Because if she couldn't handle the short scene Ian had planned, she wouldn't have a prayer of being the woman he and Gage had hoped to find.

Fighting his attraction to Holly had been an exercise in futility. And now, watching as Gage pinched her tightly pebbled nipple firmly between his fingers and gained her immediate response, he wondered just how deep her submission ran. Damn the woman was absolutely gorgeous. And even though Callie would always hold a special place in his heart, Jace had known from the first moment they'd caught her on the dock that she belonged to Ian.

He and Ian had both been perfectly clear on the boundaries of his role as the couple's *third.* Jace had always planned to find a woman to call his own, even if he shared her with Gage, he knew they would both consider her their own. From the first touch, Jace had felt an almost magnetic pull to Daphne's assistant. They had been introduced in Ian's downtown office one evening a couple of months ago when Jace had walked in just as the shy woman was leaving for the day. She had turned back to the door after bidding goodnight to Ian's executive assistant and promptly run face-first into his chest. When he'd grabbed her upper arms to keep her from falling to the floor Jace had felt a zing of electricity race from his fingers all the way up his arms and then travel like a lightning bolt straight into the deepest regions of his brain.

When he'd smiled down at her, he'd seen a flash of hesitance in her pretty green eyes just an instant before she lowered her gaze to the floor. He had noticed how nervous she seemed but he'd assumed it was because of his size. Standing six and a half feet tall with the upper body befitting his former career as a Navy SEAL he often intimidated people without even trying. He didn't maintain the same level of physical conditioning that he'd had to as a part of the teams— but he wasn't far off that mark. After Holly had excused herself and left, Jace hadn't been in Ian's office more than just a few short minutes before returning back down to the street. As he'd made his way back to his truck, he'd notice a man yelling at a woman standing next to a car in the dark shadow of the building. As he'd gotten closer he'd discovered the crying woman was Holly Mills.

As a gentleman, a Dom, and McGregor Holdings' Chief of Security, there wasn't a chance in hell he would have even considered ignoring the situation. When he'd stepped close, she had clearly been mortified to have him see her in that circumstance, but he'd been much more concerned with her safety than he had been with her embarrassment.

The distraction he'd provided by approaching had allowed her to wrench her bruised arm free from the asshole that had been holding her in his vise-like grip. She'd quickly made her way around the car that Jace was certain was a rental. Holly had assured him that she'd been fine before climbing behind the wheel and racing away. When he'd called the office the next day to check on her, he'd been told she had called in sick. He'd decided to give her a couple of days to get her bearings before he pursued the subject further. When Callie had been attacked a few days later, Jace had seen Holly at the hospital and she'd seemed fine so he'd let it go.

After Jace had returned from a lengthy trip with Ian and Callie, he'd heard that Daphne Craig had filed reports twice saying a former coworker of Holly's had been in the office and should be considered a security threat. She'd requested the man be listed on the company's list of ass hats that weren't allowed admittance. The request had caught the team's attention because the man was a well-known Broadway actor. When Jace had tried to talk to Holly she'd cancelled two different appointments and then e-mailed him begging him to let it go so that she wouldn't lose her job or attract any media attention.

Jace had thought it was odd that the young woman was concerned with bringing media attention to herself or Ian's company because neither were concerns that most employees even considered until they'd witnessed the damage the press could do. He'd assured Holly that Ian would never fire her for being a victim, but he'd be pissed as hell to find out she needed help and hadn't asked for it. Jace had been left with the impression that his words hadn't really gotten through to her, though he'd be hard pressed to explain why he'd gotten that feeling. But as every Special Ops soldier will tell you, instincts are powerful gifts and shouldn't ever be ignored.

Chapter 3

Standing just inside the main lounge looking out over the friends that had gathered to wish both she and Ian well as they started their life together, Callie's eyes were drawn to the trio standing just a few yards to their left. Leaning back into her new husband and Master's arms she reveled in the feeling of his strength surrounding her. He filled holes in her soul that she hadn't even known were there. There was no way to explain how much more complete she felt with Ian in her life. Luckily most of her new friends were also involved in Dominant/submissive relationships so she didn't have to explain it to them, they already understood.

Watching as Gage Hughes slid his hand into the top of Holly Mills's pretty halter dress was ratcheting up Callie's own arousal exponentially…something she was sure her loving Master wouldn't miss. Ian's warm breath against her ear confirmed that he had noted her response and that caused her body to react even further before her mind even caught up enough to process his words. "*Carlin*, watch as Master Jace proves to you exactly what a man of honor he is—see how his muscles twitch with the desire to touch her? This is a woman he has been watching for months, but he won't move on her because he's made a pledge to you. And until he's released from that promise, he'll honor it."

It tore at Callie's heart to know that Jace wasn't able to pursue a life and love of his own because he had promised to be their *third*. Since he was considered a permanent part of their relationship, she knew he was bound by the same pledge of fidelity that she and Ian had made to one another. The relationship could only be ended when they all agreed that it had run its course. Jace had been a strong influence on her and he'd taught her so much. They'd actually become very close friends over the past few months and she hoped what she was about to do didn't change that fact.

When his words finally penetrated the fog of lust she was floating in, she turned in his arms. "Master, could I ask you for one more gift?" Ian showered her with gifts, some large, but many were small but significant trinkets or acts that just let her know he was always listening to her. He'd bought and then helped her plant a butterfly bush outside their bedroom one afternoon because she'd mentioned how much she had loved watching them as a child. Of course he'd made sure she was naked while they'd worked, but it had still been great fun. He'd also helped her decorate their Christmas tree with old ornaments they'd purchased after a morning spent garage-saling. He'd had no idea what a garage sale was until she'd taken him one Saturday the previous fall. But in true Ian fashion, he'd quickly gotten into the spirit of things. She'd laughed until she had cried as he'd haggled with one man over a fifty-cent item. He'd ended up paying for the small ceramic angel she'd admired with a fifty dollar bill and then refused to take the change.

There had been relatively few bumps in the road for them recently, but she wasn't naïve enough to think she would ever fully understand all that being a *good sub* entailed. But Ian had assured her life would be very boring without her regular punishments for this, that, and the other.

The deep timbre of Ian's chuckle brought her back to the moment. "Carlin, I don't know where you just wandered off to, but I hope you enjoyed the trip because you just earned a few swats for not answering me—twice." When she'd first met Ian and Jace they had been amazed by what they called her little "mental road trips" and for the most part she'd gotten much better about "staying present" as Ian called it, but apparently she still had some work to do before she mastered the skill. *Well crap on a cracker, good thing swats aren't always very much of a punishment.*

She felt her face heat and knew from his indulgent smile that she must have blushed a deep red. Her damned fair complexion was a curse when it came to trying to conceal any type of embarrassment. "I'm sorry, Master. I got lost in the memories of our garage sale day and all of the thousand other ways you've made me feel special. Could you repeat the question, please?"

"Very well said, my love, you'll still get the swats, but I believe I might just change the purpose a bit." His fingers were trailing gently down the side of her face and that simple touch soothed her and she found herself leaning into his touch without even thinking about it. She pushed her cheek into the comfort of his palm and listened as his voice settled her even further. "Now, my beautiful wife, tell me what your heart desires."

She took a deep breath and decided to just spit it out. She'd always promised herself she would never be the kind of wife who was afraid to speak her mind with her spouse and she figured that now was as good a time as any to begin. "I'd like Master Jace released from our agreement so he can pursue his own happiness." She knew her words hadn't come out as eloquently as she'd intended, but they had been spoken from her heart. "Don't get me wrong, I love Master Jace, but I'm not *in love* with him. My heart will always treasure his time with us, but it belongs wholly to you." *Pickle fudge, every time I try to sound articulate and educated I end up sounding like a Romper-Room reject.*

* * * *

For the first time in days Callie was actually acting like herself again and Ian was more relieved than he wanted to admit. She had been so withdrawn and subdued recently that he'd actually been worried about whether or not she would go through with the wedding.

And hearing her speaking her thoughts aloud again had been music to his ears. Not only were those musings pure insight into how her mind worked, they were also inevitably opportunities to get to the bottom of her concerns. Not to mention the fact that most often they were joy-filled and often funny as hell. He knew her pregnancy was weighing heavily on her mind, but when he'd asked her if she was having second thoughts she'd assured him she was thrilled. She'd told him that everything inside her felt out of balance and she didn't understand it all. Her obstetrician had assured them both her feelings were perfectly normal but that didn't stop him from worrying about her.

While he and Jace had been on the stage with Callie for her collaring ceremony earlier this evening, Ian had noted his friend's gaze tracking Holly's presence at the back of the room. After the ceremony Ian had intentionally brought Callie back into the room this way in hopes this very opportunity would present itself. He agreed with her that Jace needed to be free to chase his own happiness and he had a feeling that race had already begun.

He leaned down and kissed Callie and then turned her around so she could watch the scene play out while he talked her to orgasm. One of the things he and Jace had discovered about his new bride was that she enjoyed watching and she even liked being watched now that she didn't fear Senator Westmore. The man and his wife had plotted and schemed to destroy Callie's name and reputation in order to discredit her, and their years of abuse had taken a toll on her.

Callie had been raped by the good senator's son and one of his friends when she'd been a teenager. Her mother had basically thrown her to the wolves so that she could gain financially from the situation and Callie had supported her sister for years before Ian had discovered the sister's deception and put a stop to it. He was collecting the sister's repayments and distributing the money to local charities in Callie's name. His soft-hearted sub hadn't wanted anything to do with the money, but Ian hadn't been willing to let her vicious sister get away with her betrayal. After the senator's wife attacked Callie in a dress shop, the lunatic was distracted enough by her own legal battles that she was leaving Callie alone for the moment. Seeing Callie begin putting all of that heartache behind her had been one of Ian's greatest joys.

Ian still hadn't decided exactly how to exact revenge on the woman who had hurt the most important person in his world, but he certainly hadn't given up on the idea either. Ian didn't ordinarily consider himself a vengeful person, but Nanette Westmore had earned his wrath. As for the senator, he'd lost his Senate seat when his wife had been recorded discussing his Alzheimer's diagnosis and bragging about how her mob-boss father had been calling the shots for her ailing husband for the past several years. Surprisingly the scandal hadn't damaged the club or his businesses and he was quite sure that was largely due to the incredible management skills of Daphne Craig, his executive assistant. The woman had been on top of the press from the moment the incident had occurred and she'd been relentless in feeding the media every sound bite she could that painted the Westmores as tainted and Callie as the pure ray of sunlight that she was.

Callie's coworkers at the small tabloid where she had worked had also been a huge help. They hadn't been aware that Ian had actually been their employer until after the incident and he'd quickly promoted each one of her friends who had stepped up to vouch for her. He'd bought the small paper months ago because he'd grown tired of them continually trying to get information on his club. He had intended to find out who was responsible for their relentless pursuit, and it had quickly played out when Callie had been, for all intents and purposes, blackmailed into accepting the assignment. She'd been tasked with sneaking onto the island to gather information. Capturing the tiny cat burglar had been the luckiest moment of Ian's life.

Watching Gage bend forward, effectively wrapping his body around the woman in his arms, was the prelude to what his friend had planned and Ian was going to enjoy taking Callie along for the ride. He mirrored Gage's posture and slid his hand into Callie's dress and pinched her tightly budded nipple until she gasped and then groaned as the pain quickly morphed into pleasure. "Watch as Master Gage speaks close to her ear just as I'm doing to you. See how her chest rises and falls quickly as her breathing spikes? Her body is flooding itself with oxygen as it readies itself for climax. Gage has his face pressed against her neck so he can feel how her heart is pounding in anticipation of his touch. He knows her sex is swelling as blood rushes to her pussy and he's giving her body the opportunity to enjoy the anticipation." Ian slid his hands up the front hem of her dress knowing she was bare to his touch. Sliding his fingers through her slick folds and skillfully encircling her clit, he coaxed it out from its protective hood.

Ian was certain that he could take Callie up the mountain of arousal faster than Gage was going to go with Holly simply because his wife already trusted him and was amazingly responsive. He'd discovered early in their time together just how easily she slipped into sub-space. Most subs needed time and either pain or pleasure, but Callie was capable of attaining that level of submission from his voice alone.

Ian hadn't believed he would ever find a woman he could truly love. After the pain and betrayal he had experienced at the hands of his stepmother, he had decided all women only cared about money and sex—and in that order. Nolyn McGregor, not Nolyn Bieberle, had introduced Ian to the world of BDSM when he had been a young teenager. And her promises to leave his father for him had been as empty as all the promises she'd made to the numerous other rich young men she'd been playing with while driving a wedge between Ian and his father. That wedge had just started to fall to the wayside when his father died of a heart attack much too young. Ian had been just days from graduating from college and instead of pursuing his own dreams, he'd been called home to head up a company that was teetering on the verge of financial collapse. If it hadn't been for the wise counsel of longtime family friend, Daniel Lamont, things might well have turned out much differently.

Jace Garrett was his best friend in the entire world and watching him stand like a statue in front of the woman Ian knew had captured his interest was as sad as it was sexually stimulating. And feeling his wife's pussy flood with her sweet cream as she got closer and closer to another mind-blowing orgasm was about as good as life got for a Dom.

Chapter 4

Gage spoke softly against Holly's small ear and smiled when he felt her entire body shiver, "Do you like having Master Jace watching you, sweetheart? Open those beautiful green eyes, baby. Can you see the desire in his eyes? Oh, Master Jace, I believe our sweet girl likes knowing what she's doing to you because her whole body just shook with her desire and I can smell her arousal."

Gage was certain Holly had forgotten that he had actually asked her two questions and he was just getting ready to demand a response when he heard her breathy answer. "Yes...yes to both questions. He said I couldn't, but I do." Gage had damned well understood the first thing she'd said, but the second was a complete mystery and judging by the confused expression he saw on Jace's face, his friend didn't know what she'd meant either.

Holly's head had fallen back against Gage's shoulder and for the first time in as long as he could remember, he was actually grateful for a sub's failure to follow an instruction because it gave him a chance to get the go ahead from Jace. At his friend's signal to proceed, Gage leaned down and bit just hard enough at the tender place where Holly's neck met her shoulder to get her attention. When she jerked her head back up, her eyes wide and glazed over with her arousal, Gage had to suppress his smile. "That's right, sweetie, you need to keep those beautiful emerald eyes focused on Master Jace. No matter what I do to you, I don't want you to look away from him, do you understand?"

Gage would have bet she hadn't heard a word he'd said because her breathing was little more than shallow pants and he felt her heart pounding against the hand he had splayed over her chest. Being so tall was a definite advantage at times like this because he was able to reach around her with his other hand and slide it up under her dress until he was at the top of her panties. Slipping his fingers under the elastic and feeling the lace rasp against his knuckles he groaned as his fingers slid over her bare mound. God in heaven, if there was one thing he loved on a woman it was a waxed pussy and Holly Mills was completely bare to his touch—and touch he did. He slipped his fingers through the soaking folds all the way to the tight rosette at the back and whispered, "Oh sweetie, you just made me a very happy man indeed. I wish Master Jace could see your waxed pussy because he'd be as turned on by it as I am." He felt her body tremble and knew she was getting closer.

"Open your legs a little further for me sweetheart. I want to feel each and every one of the soft petals of your soaking sex. You are so wet for me and I am very pleased by the feeling of my fingers gliding effortlessly through your nether lips." He felt a fresh wash of her syrup roll over his fingers as he spoke to her. The small bud of her clit was peeking out from under its hood and when he gave it a gentle squeeze her felt her begin to shake. He was glad he had both of his arms wrapped around her so all he had to do was tighten his grip, because he was sure her legs weren't going to hold her much longer. And the Dom in him was pleased more than he'd admit that he was going to knock her right off her feet.

"Tell Master Jace how wet you are for me, Holly." He heard Jace groan and knew there was going to be hell to pay for torturing his friend, but fuck it, Jace was the one who had sent Gage to *secure* her, so in Gage's view that set the stage for the scene playing out now. Gage heard Jace growl what sounded a lot like "*fuck me*" and worried that his own voice had been too abrasive for a woman he had barely ever even spoken to.

He felt her knees begin to sag so he gave her pussy a small swat, and nearly came when her words immediately started to tumble out.

"Master Jace, my pussy is very wet and the feel of Master Gage's fingers sliding all the way from the front to the back is making me want to come more than I want my next breath. He was wrong, I'm so happy he was wrong, because this feels so good." Gage had been fighting off his own release and he wanted to attribute his confusion over her words to the fact that his brain was being forced to function with a minimum supply of oxygen since all his blood was currently residing between his navel and his knees. He needed to get this moving along before he bent her over, tore her lacy little panties off that smooth pussy and fucked her until they were both sated—and God only knew how long that would take.

Glancing to his right, Gage noted Ian and Callie standing just a few feet away. From what he could tell Ian was mirroring his actions and using the scene to feed his sweet sub's voyeuristic kink. Since he didn't know how Holly would react to being watched he wasn't going to draw her attention to her boss and his new wife. He'd just keep Holly's attention on Jace and they'd save the questions about her hard and soft limits for later—a lot later.

"Don't take your eyes off Master Jace, sweetness. Tonight is about your pleasure, but I won't let you be a bratty sub either. If you close your eyes or look away, he'll tell me and then I'll have to paddle your beautiful ass, and that isn't how I want tonight to play out. Oh no, baby girl, I want my hands all over you, but first I want to feel you come apart in my arms." Holly Mills was probably the sexiest woman he'd held in his arms since he and a few of the others in Ian's trusted circle had helped him with a punishment scene for Callie a few months ago. But that had been entirely different because everyone had always known that Callie's heart and soul belonged to Ian. But Holly was reacting to both he and Jace and he wondered to himself if perhaps she might be the *one* they'd been hoping to find.

Jace pulled her small curvy body even tighter against his chest and just as he felt her body start to convulse in his arms he bit down on her shoulder again and growled. "Come for us, Holly." He heard her low-pitched scream just as he felt his fingers being flooded with her cum. He couldn't wait until he could feel her come over his tongue as he fucked her with it and curled it up to scrap over the sensitive spot he'd felt with his fingers. One scrape of his callused finger over her G-spot and she'd gone off like a rocket. Gage's only regret was that he hadn't been able to see her eyes as she'd climaxed, but from the look on Jace's face it must have been spectacular.

Gage scooped Holly up into his arms and was quickly making his way toward one of the smaller sitting areas at the back of the main lounge when he heard Ian call out to Jace. Gage didn't stop to see what their boss wanted because he knew it wouldn't be a long discussion. Ian had given his tiny sub her own screaming orgasm so he'd be anxious to provide her with a few minutes of downtime before returning to their guests. That was Gage's plan as well, because proper aftercare was essential following a scene, and particularly so for less experienced submissives because the emotional overload often led to a crash while coming back down from the high. Until subs understood that *the crash* was perfectly normal, it could be very unsettling and frightening.

Settling down on a leather sofa, Gage cuddled Holly to his chest and just took in the musky scent of her arousal which was overpowering the citrus scent of her shampoo. In a few minutes he'd show her to the ladies' locker room where he knew she would find anything and everything she might need to freshen up before they joined the party. But for the next few minutes he wanted to give her a chance to come back to earth. He'd let her get her bearings and then there were several things the three of them needed to discuss. He hoped Jace would join them before she started asking questions. He knew they would start—there wasn't any doubt about that—but at the moment, he wasn't sure exactly how to answer them. He knew he and Jace needed to present a united front with Holly if they planned to share her at all.

* * * *

Jace stood in front of his best friend and one of the sweetest women he'd ever met, too stunned to speak. When he'd first heard Ian's voice calling him over, he'd been tempted to ignore his friend and continue following Gage and Holly. But there had been something in Ian's tone that had told Jace he wasn't going to be willing to back off. When he'd nodded his head toward his office, Jace had wanted to roll his eyes because this evidently wasn't going to be a quick conversation.

When they had all three sat on the leather sofa in Ian's office, he'd pulled Callie's tiny feet into his lap as he usually did during aftercare and rubbed them gently. When she looked up at him he'd seen tears swimming in her pretty eyes and he'd felt his heart clench. If she'd seen the scene then it was likely she'd seen how fiercely he'd had to fight his desire to touch Holly, and if he'd hurt Callie he was going to feel like a real asshole. She must have seen the regret in his eyes because her expression cleared immediately and she quickly scrambled onto his lap. She placed her hands on the sides of his face, "Jace, I want you to do something for all of us." When the little imp looked at him, he could suddenly see the mischief that was always just below the surface with her. "And after all, it's my wedding day…so you can't very well deny me this one simple request."

He was having trouble not telling her to just get on with it, but he decided she was right, there was very little he'd ever be able to deny her when it came right down to it. They had become very close over the past few months and even though he wasn't *in love* with her, he loved her. It felt something like his feelings for his younger sister, Abby—but then again, *definitely not.*

The little minx stroked her fingers through his hair at his temples, a move she knew he found immensely relaxing, and as usual he closed his eyes, lost in the pure pleasure of her touch. He jerked his eyes open when he heard Ian's chuckle, "Carlin, you better continue or you're going to start something you aren't going to be willing to finish."

Callie shook her head as if her Master's words had brought her back to the present. Jace almost laughed out loud at her bright pink blush. How she could still manage to blush after all he and Ian had taught her was a testament to what a good person she was. But anyone who underestimated the tiny blonde, as he had that first night, was going to find out the hard way why Ian had nicknamed her *Carlin* because she more than lived up to the Irish name meaning "little warrior."

Ian was shocked by Callie's next words, "Please go after the woman you are so obviously interested in. I'll miss you as our third, but what kind of a friend would I be if I stood between you and the happiness that you so richly deserve?" Callie leaned forward and kissed him on the cheek. "Just promise me you'll still be my friend and confidant, even if you aren't our third any longer. Because, Master Jace, you and I both know I need all the help and guidance I can get." Her sweet smile squeezed his heart.

God Almighty he was glad Ian had found Callie because she had been a saving grace for both of them. She'd come into their lives when Jace had decided there wasn't a woman out there worth their salt. He'd been burned once too often and had decided that commitment might not be in his future despite his and Gage's hope to find a special woman to share. Ian had been antsy for months before Callie's less than stealthy arrival in the middle of the night, and everyone around him had been worried about him. But everything seemed to fall immediately into place from the first moment Ian touched her, the sense of peace that had fallen over him had been almost palpable.

Thinking back on that night and how "Calamity Callie" had fallen, banged around, and cursed out at the end of the dock still made Jace chuckle. He and Ian had been completely blown away by the little blonde sprite from that first encounter, and her friendship would always be a treasure Jace held close to his heart.

"Sweetness, there isn't an explosive made that could destroy our friendship. It will always be one of my most valuable possessions." He paused to hug her tiny frame close to his chest. When he looked up at his best friend, he saw nothing in Ian's eyes but love and compassion. Lifting her easily and settling her back onto Ian's lap, Jace stroked his fingers slowly down the side of her elfin face. She was such an amazing contrast of fragile and strong and the combination was further enhanced by her sweet spirit.

But, as excited and happy as he was for his best friend, Jace knew it was time to chase his own happiness. There was just something about Holly Mills that called to him, where exactly it would lead them was anyone's guess, but it was certainly time to find out.

Chapter 5

The sadness Jace had expected to feel at the idea of stepping away from being the *third* for Ian and Callie didn't materialize and he was certain that was mostly due to the anticipation he felt about finally being able to pursue a relationship with the curvy little brunette who had captured his interest so many months ago. Rounding the corner into the small sitting area he had been sure Gage would use, his heart stuttered at the sight of Holly curled in Gage's lap. Jace sat down on the small loveseat and was happy to see the soft subbie blanket his friend had wrapped her in was tucked around her loosely enough that he could easily slide his hands inside and pull her legs across his lap.

He felt her stiffen, but held her calves firmly in his large hands. He felt Gage's gaze on him and when he looked up into his friend's eyes he could see the silent question there. At his nod, Gage seemed to relax, knowing that everything with Ian and Callie had obviously been resolved. Both men were firm believers in loyalty and fidelity. Their Texas upbringings and values their families had instilled were still rock solid despite the fact neither of them had lived in the Lone Star state for many years.

"Holly, I want you to know that Ian and Callie have released me from our agreement. If I was still their *third* I wouldn't be touching you. I want you to understand that as long as you, Gage, and I are exploring the attraction we're all feeling we won't touch another woman unless our jobs at the club require it for some reason." Even though she was looking at him, he wasn't entirely convinced she was fully focused on his words yet.

"Pet, I need you to focus on me for a moment, can you do that?" He watched as her eyes seemed to clear for a moment just before they filled with tears. He watched, completely stunned as the tears ran in streams down her cheeks. Glancing up at Gage he could tell that he was just as baffled. "Holly, tell us why you are crying." Jace let enough of his Dom tone ring through the command that she would know he wasn't going to let it go, but he also knew that she would have heard the compassion and sincerity as well. She shifted her gaze between the two of them quickly before dropping her eyes to her lap, but still hadn't answered. Jace lifted her chin with his fingers so she was forced to look at him. "Right now, Holly, or we'll have to take you to one of the private rooms and deal with your misbehavior. And since this is our first chance to really have a conversation, that isn't how either Master Gage or I would prefer this to go."

Gage moved her face to his own and raised a brow. "Sweetheart, don't make us punish you right out of the gate. Much as I can barely contain myself thinking about getting my hands on your sweet ass, I would rather your memories of tonight are not of us paddling an answer out of you."

"I'm sorry, I just got lost in thought for a bit. It's been so long since anyone actually *saw* me that I…well, I was overwhelmed at the feeling of it for a bit, you know?" For the life of him, Jace couldn't figure out what she'd just said. Hell, it had sounded like English, but it hadn't made any sense whatsoever.

Gage looked at him and shrugged, "I don't have a fucking clue what she just said, but something about it makes me think somewhere along the line this little beauty has been sold a bill of goods about her value. And the part that chafes my ass is that she seems to have bought into it hook, line, and sinker." Jace knew Gage as well as anyone, and there was no doubt in his mind that his friend was only half kidding. Both Jace and Gage were like the other Doms at Club Isola who believed that protecting their submissives meant not only looking out for their physical needs, but meeting their emotional needs as well. None of them had any patience with abuse, no matter what form it was presented in. Gage continued looking at Holly and then lowered his tone. "Sweetness, you need to clarify your statement. You're dealing with a couple of country boys here, and well darlin'— sometimes we can be a bit thick." The only thing thick about Gage Hughes was his Texas accent when he decided to let it out in full force. As a Special Forces operative, Gage had been trained in two other languages and had actually become fluent in several others as well, so his accent was usually nowhere to be heard. But, if it suited his purpose, he could call it forth in a heartbeat.

Jace looked at Holly's wide-eyed look and nearly laughed out loud. "Pet, try that answer again. This time, make sure you aren't just thinking out loud." If he'd had to guess, he would have to assume she had answered the question aloud, but her answer sounded more like she'd been speaking to herself than to them. He could only hope that he and Gage would be as lucky as Ian and their woman would think out loud. God he and Ian had enjoyed Callie's little *mental road trips* as they'd referred to them, because she had often narrated the journeys so they had been able to easily figure out what she had been thinking most of the time. Lately she'd seemed to only lapse into that when she was particularly stressed or tired. He and Ian had both commented how much they missed listening to the quirky way her mind processed information.

The puzzled look on Holly's face was adorable, but she seemed to clue in quickly and for the first time, Jace saw a glimmer of spirit in her pretty green eyes. "Oh, well okay. I'll be happy to explain, but just so you know, I'm not buying that lame *country boy* routine at all. I know you are both former Special Forces and since I've had friends in various branches of the military's special teams, I am well aware of how bright you have to be to get into the SEALS and Rangers."

Both Jace and Gage blinked at her in surprise and then burst out laughing. Jace recovered first so he was the one to respond, "Well, my sweet pet, I don't know why I'm startled to find out how well-informed and articulate you are when I should have known you would be. Hell, anyone who works in Ian's executive offices has to be the cream of the crop. And impressing Daphne Craig would be even harder than performing satisfactorily for Ian. So, on behalf of Gage and myself, I'll ask you to forgive us for assuming that excuse would fly. And I assure you we'll come up with something better to cover up our intellectual failings in the future."

She rolled her eyes at him—she honest to God rolled her eyes. Granted he had been teasing her, but rolling your eyes at a Dom was never a good plan and she'd just done it to both of them *and* inside a BDSM club during what was awfully close to a scene. Jace knew Gage would have seen it and was likely as incredulous as he was. When Gage quickly moved her arms so that he'd shackled her wrists in one of his hands behind her back, Jace did the same with her ankles.

Gage pressed his lips so close to her ear that Jace didn't doubt Holly could feel his breath like a warm breeze pushing over the shell with each word he spoke. "Holly, rolling your eyes at us just earned you a punishment for a couple of reasons. First of all, even though Master Jace was teasing you, he and I are both still Doms. Rolling your eyes at Doms is *never* a good idea. Also, you are inside a BDSM club. I don't know exactly what you know about the lifestyle, but there are some fairly well-established guidelines that are followed and you're about to get a small taste of it."

Jace watched as several emotions passed over Holly's face. First he'd seen frustration, then fear which had quickly morphed into arousal. Jace slid his free hand up the inside of her thigh and began teasing her through the lace of her panties. The scrap of fabric might be covering her pussy, but the rasp of his fingers pushing it over her sensitive labia was quickly pushing her right to the edge. "Keep in mind there are several types of punishments, my pet. Since this is your first offense, we're going to be a bit creative, but the next time you roll your eyes at a Dom, we'll have your bare ass over a spanking bench and glowing bright red before you can blink. Now spread your legs and lean back against Master Gage's arm." He released one of her ankles so that she could comply and she slowly moved her legs apart, but just barely. "Further, don't be shy now, pet. You've earned this punishment and you'll take it with dignity and grace, and you'll be grateful the club isn't in full operation tonight or we'd be doing this up on the stage for everyone to see."

Jace knew he'd just reminded Holly that they weren't in a private setting and that they would be clearly visible to anyone rounding the corner. Bringing her attention back to him, he added, "Your only job is to do as you're told, pet. Let us worry about who sees you. You can trust that we'll never do anything to hurt you and we'll always give you exactly what you need." It went unsaid that what she needed and what she wanted would often not be even remotely the same, but that was a discussion they'd have another time.

* * * *

Holly's head was spinning so quickly she was worried she might actually lose her balance and fall from Gage's lap. The minute they'd mentioned punishing her, her entire body had gone on high alert. Oh, she wasn't afraid of them, quite the opposite in fact. She wouldn't admit it to them, but she was actually something of an adrenaline junkie. Holly had discovered at a fairly young age that her sexual gratification and an *edge* of some type were tied together in ways she'd never been able to understand or explain. And despite the fact that she'd been writing about it for years, she'd rarely actually experienced it.

She worried that once these two experienced Doms found out just how little personal exposure she'd had to their world, they'd decide there were too many better choices available and she'd be yesterday's news before she knew what hit her. That realization solidified her commitment to *seizing the moment* so she slid her legs apart as far as she could without falling off Gage's lap. When he lifted his leg so that it rested on the table in front of the loveseat he'd settled them on, she realized he was making sure she wasn't in danger of sliding out of his hold.

"Sweetheart, spread your legs further apart. Don't worry, I'm not going to let you fall. You'll always be safe in our care." When she looked up into his eyes, it was clear that he'd meant every word he'd spoken, but she wasn't sure he realized how easily she could be hurt by them both. She'd been hiding out working as an administrative assistant for her Aunt Daphne for several months, even though no one at McGregor Holdings, except Ian, had any idea they were related. Daphne, according to Holly's mother, had always been a force of nature and Holly had known working for her would be anything but a cake walk. But Holly had thrown herself into the work and had been pleased when her ultra-organized aunt had quickly recognized they were kindred work spirits.

Holly knew her time at McGregor was limited. Hell's bells, she'd already been spotted by one of the actors she'd worked with and he'd been a royal pain in her ass for weeks until she had finally convinced him that she would come to him personally as soon as she was ready to return to Broadway with the completed manuscript he'd gotten a glimpse of before she'd pulled her disappearing act. No one understood the stress she'd been under until she'd broken, because no one knew *everything*. Working as a screenwriter and playwright under a pseudonym had been difficult enough, but then she'd done a couple of small roles as an actress and used a different name for that to protect her other two identities. When you added that to the novels she had written and that she spent a lot of her free time promoting those while she was gathering information for the next installment in the series, it probably shouldn't have been a surprise that it had finally become too much.

The different titles and roles had eventually become a nightmare of deception and personality changes that would have made Sybil proud. Wishing she had stuck with either acting or writing was a moot point now, all she could do was hope that she had a few more weeks to enjoy the pleasure of anonymity before she was thrown headfirst back into the lion's den.

Holly Mills would always be who she really was at her core. She'd loved her time as a writer because it allowed her to be anonymous. And hiding from the world after disastrous experiences in both boarding school and college was an easy path to follow. When it had become obvious to her that she was becoming too comfortable as a recluse, she'd accepted an invitation to act. But working as an actress had been a soul-sucking experience from hell. If she never stepped foot on a stage again it would be fine by her. Oh, it wasn't that it was difficult work, it was just mind numbing and off-the-chart boring. At least she'd had the scripts she'd been working on to keep her busy during the ridiculous amount of downtime she'd had between scenes, but it had been crystal clear to her how many actors got so derailed from their roots and sent over the edge into various kinds of addictions. The boredom accompanied by the outrageous amounts of money and the pressure to look and act perfect *all the time* were bound to make even the strongest people crack eventually.

One of Holly's biggest weaknesses had always been the fact she could let her mind out for a short little break and it wouldn't come back until after dark...or at least that was what her father had always claimed. She'd always figured he had every right to make the observation since he was one of the most creative but distractible people she'd ever known. Sighing to herself, she thought again how much her life had changed since she'd moved out of her parents' palatial home. Her mom had gotten increasingly more demanding and even though her dad was a nice man...and God knew he had to be to put up with her mother...Holly could see that her mother was steadily draining all the creative energy right out of him. Eventually her dad would end up being dull and boring just like her mother, and those were two traits Holly had never found attractive in a man.

Chapter 6

Gage glanced up at Jace and smiled. Jesus, Joseph, and Mary how did they get so lucky to get a woman like Callie who mentally rambled—*Aloud?* Oh yes, indeed, they'd been blessed for sure. Jace hadn't moved a muscle since they'd situated her with her legs spread wide and Gage knew his friend well enough that there wasn't any doubt it had to be killing him to have a full view of Holly's pussy and not be fully enjoying all it had to offer. She'd said several things he'd found troubling, first of all was some reference to an actor she'd worked with having bothered her for weeks and then something about someone named Sybil.

It had been obvious the second she came back into the moment because she'd gone completely rigid in his arms. Gage's best guess was that she was wondering if she'd been speaking out loud—*Oh indeed you have, sweetheart*—and if so, how many of her secrets had just spilled—*not nearly enough, but Master Jace and I intend to uncover each and every one.*

"Well, now that you seemed to have rejoined us, sweetness, I want to tell you that from this point forward there will be consequences for your mental road trips. It's important for many reasons that you stay with us when we're in a scene, and don't doubt for a moment that this is a scene. Chief among those reasons is your safety, but we'll explain more about that as we go—suffice to say, we need to know you are processing what is happening at that moment and that you aren't reacting to something that happened to you before or something you are worried about in the future. We'll explore both ends of that spectrum with you because they will likely affect the way you react to scenes, but *during* a scene, you need to be present and accounted for. Do you understand, Holly?"

Gage had been slowly running his fingers from her temple down through her long dark hair enjoying the feel of the silken strands as they slid through his fingers. He could feel her body shift from the muscle tension that accompanies fear and worry to the tension that accompanies sexual arousal. The shift was subtle, but it had been unmistakable. He'd seen it before with exceptionally bright women or he might not have recognized it.

"Now, we *are* planning to play with you a bit before I seat you on my aching cock, but I think you'll be waiting a bit for that release your body is going to be craving as soon as Master Jace begins working his magic between your lovely thighs." The smell of her arousal hit him like a blast and when he saw Jace's smile, he knew his friend was enjoying the intoxicating aroma as well. Gage knew Jace would be able to push Holly to the edge with just a few well-placed strokes, and he also knew she wasn't going to be able to hold back her release even though he was going to command her to do just that. Holding off an orgasm was a learned skill and usually took many years to perfect. Many women struggled to reach their release, so it was counterintuitive for them to step away from it willingly.

Licking the shell of her ear before he pulled the lobe between his teeth and sucked on it with a pressure he wanted her to realize was the beginning of his dominance over her, he spoke against her warm skin, "Don't come until one of us gives you permission to do so, sweetheart. If you do, you're going to be turned over my knee and spanked. Do you understand my instruction?" When she didn't respond immediately he added, "Make sure you speak your answers—immediately and in complete honesty, always. Oh, and lying by omission is still lying, sweetness."

Her soft gasp went straight to his cock which was already straining for release from its denim prison. But it was her whispered, "Yes, I understand…please touch me." That nearly sent him over the edge. Jesus, he hadn't lost control since he'd been in high school. How the hell had this untrained sub gotten under his skin so quickly? What was it about her that seemed to speak directly to his soul? Was the fragility he sensed beneath the surface real or imagined? Giving himself a mental shake, he refocused his attention on the women in his arms. Seeing the almost imperceptible nod from Jace, Gage turned Holly's face to his own and ran his tongue over her lips in a soft caress. When she opened to him, he dove in with unrestrained enthusiasm, exploring all the hidden places and mentally noting each and every reaction.

When Holly moved her hands to his face he moved both of them behind her back and shackled both of her small wrists easily with one hand. He wanted to shout for joy when her entire body arched toward him as she responded to the bondage. *Oh, you like being restrained don't you little one? Master Jace and I are going to love exploring that with you.* Just as the thought ran through his mind, Gage heard Jace's growl. "Oh, I do believe you like being restrained, don't you pet? We'll be happy to show you all the ways we can use bondage so that your lovely body is ours to do with as we please. You'll be at our mercy, baby, will you enjoy that?"

Gage pulled back from the kiss so that she could answer Jace's question, but from her dazed look, he wasn't sure she was going to be able to focus enough to form words. He was surprised when she closed her eyes and moaned her assent. "Open your eyes. Don't ever hide from us. There will be times we'll blindfold you to minimize your distractions or to help you focus your attention on the sensations we're creating, but until we do, you'll keep your eyes open so we can see all of those lovely shades of green as they change with the emotions racing through you, sweet sub."

* * * *

Jace Garrett wasn't sure he'd ever seen anything that aroused him as much as Holly Mills arching her back in response to Gage clamping his hand around her delicate wrists. Jace had worried when he'd seen Gage remove her fingers from his hair and move them behind her back that perhaps his friend was pushing Holly too fast. Gage was one of the strictest Doms Jace had ever known. The man's style of Dominance was a total contrast to the laid-back Texan persona that most people saw. They still hadn't gotten the answer they'd originally been after, but somehow, Jace had the idea it was all going to come out in the next few minutes.

Jace had rarely seen more than a spark of interest in his friend's eyes when it came to a submissive they were playing with. Oh, that didn't mean the man wasn't totally focused on the task at hand, because Gage was an incredibly intuitive Dom. But because Gage was so intuitive, he knew within the first few moments of a scene whether or not it was going to work. What surprised Jace was that Callie was the only other women he'd ever seen Gage react so strongly to. Even more surprising was the fact that Jace also sensed there were many similarities between the two women. It was almost as if they were light and dark mirror images of one another.

When Gage had pulled Holly into a scorching kiss, Jace had been so absorbed in watching the hot scene playing out, he'd nearly forgotten what was right in front of him. Looking down at Holly's pussy glistening with the evidence of her arousal had made him want to shed his pants and good sense and just shove his aching cock as deep as he could in her warm, wet folds. Stroking his large fingers over the swollen petals framing her opening was akin to pressing into warm honey. Each movement he made seemed to elicit a deeper response until she was wiggling and pressing into his touch, and he could hear the slurping sounds of his fingers as they fucked her with slow, deliberate strokes.

Watching her body flush bright pink with arousal and smelling her as her silky cream ran over his hand, Jace realized that for the first time in years he was battling to maintain his own control. Feeling perspiration beading on his forehead he knew they either had to wrap this up and rejoin to the party or move to one of the private rooms. And even though he'd like nothing more than to feel her naked body pressed against his bare chest as her pussy walls squeezed his cock with the same fervor that it was using to clench his fingers, now wasn't the time or the place. That sort of full-on fucking was going to have to wait a bit.

When Gage broke the kiss, Jace reached up with this free hand and slid his palm around the base of her neck pulling her up until her forehead was resting against his own. Seeing her eyes go wide when she noticed his cock already jutting proudly from his pants, sheathed and ready, he was pleased to see her pupils dilate with desire. *Oh, no my sweet little sub, you know you are mine, don't you. You were mine from the moment you ran into my chest in Ian's office. The moment I touched you, I owned you.*

Jace pulled her over his lap. "Ride me, pet. Take me into your sweet body." Her inner tissues were swollen with her arousal and that combined with the fact she obviously hadn't had sex in a long time made her very tight. When he finally sank in deep, he felt her rotate her hips abrading her clit with the hair above his root. The rotation of her hips nearly sent him over the edge and he'd barely begun. Pushing his hands under her dress he placed them on either side of her hips and used them to help her lift herself up and down his length. Knowing he wouldn't last long, he rotated his own hips so that the next stroke pressed against the soft spot at the front of her channel that he knew would send her over quickly. Just as he felt the first flutters of her orgasm he commanded her release, "Come for us, pet." As she drew in a bracing breath, Gage reached from behind her, pinching her peaked nipples and Jace sealed his lips over hers and caught her scream. Her juices flowed over him and her pussy clamped down on his cock with contractions that seemed as though they were almost synchronized in their timing and intensity. God almighty, fucking her was a dream come true. She was responsive and her submission was bone-deep, but he knew her sharp mind was going to ensure that they earned each and every bit of her heart.

Seeing her release wash over her expression he knew the exact moment the first wave crested, so he used two fingers to pinch her pulsing clit and send her over again. He kept his mouth over hers and was grateful for Gage's arms holding her still so that he could contain her passion-filled cries. He knew they would have been bouncing off the rock walls of the vast natural cavern that housed Club Isola. He could hardly wait to hear each and every sound she made in orgasm, he just wasn't of the mind to share it during his best friend and boss's wedding reception. He let his own release rocket up out of him and that sent her over a third time, and the deep moan that he was sure must have come from her soul was the sweetest thing he'd ever heard.

Feeling Holly slowly deflate he finally broke the kiss and heard her gasping for air even as he was struggling to catch his own breath because he wasn't sure that she hadn't sucked every last bit of oxygen right out of his lungs. Looking into the emerald-green eyes that were now awash with unshed tears, Jace smiled at her because he was sure the tears were a reaction to the intensity of the emotion rather than sadness. But he'd never been one to assume he was foolproof at reading a woman's emotions, so he kissed her on the tip of her nose and asked, "Are those tears of joy or sadness, pet?"

Jace knew that neither he nor Gage had been surprised by a woman during aftercare very often, but Holly's words left him feeling as if someone had unceremoniously yanked the rug out from under him. "I don't really know. I've never experienced anything like that before. The intensity of it...the shear *knock you to your knees* wave of emotion...well, I wasn't prepared for it. Um...well, I'm sorry if I've made you uncomfortable by being so blunt. I'll just..." Jace finally realized she had moved off him and was struggling to stand up between his legs and Gage, who had been standing behind her. He and Gage had been so floored by her honesty and insightful answer that neither of them had done a thing to stop her.

Finally, years of training as a Dominant seemed to kick in and he wrapped his hand around her wrist to keep her from stepping around Gage. "Hold on, pet. Where's the fire?" She looked up and blinked at him and this time there was no question that her tears were from a gut-wrenching sadness. Instinct kicked in and Jace found himself flailing in a blinding sea of emotion that centered on protecting the beauty he held in his firm grasp. And even though it startled him, he couldn't seem to fight back the wave of need he felt when it came to Holly.

Turning her so she was facing Gage, he let his friend hold her in his arms while he quickly disposed of the condom and set his clothing right. And then pulling her carefully from Gage's arms, he settled her on his lap, making sure that she was once again covered. Gage sat once again so that he was facing her. Jace knew his quick actions had surprised her, but she had only let out a quick gasp of surprise and that earned her points for poise and grace, as his sweet mama would say. "Pet, tell me why you thought it was necessary to skedaddle off my lap as if it was on fire all of the sudden." He paused for a few seconds because the look on her startled face told him she had every intention of editing her response. "And I'm going to remind you that we'll always expect your answers to be completely honest and forthright, so don't hold back pieces of the truth because that will be a quick ticket to a paddling."

He saw the war her mind was waging because each and every emotion played itself out in brilliant Technicolor in her expression. Studying her closely he could almost see her pulling strength up from the depths of her soul as she struggled to put her feelings into words she thought they would find acceptable. One of the first skills every Special Forces soldier learns is patience, whether it's patience with themselves or someone else. It was a skill you either learned quickly or you didn't make the cut or you died quickly in the field. He could feel Gage go still beside him and knew his friend had slipped into the *wait-mode* that was as much a part of them as breathing.

Silence was his and Gage's friend, they'd been trained to not let it intimidate them. That wasn't to say that the skill wasn't a hard-earned one, because it was—particularly for Dominants who, by their very nature, were accustomed to demanding and getting answers and compliance quickly. But this was one of those moments that Jace was very grateful for all of Uncle Sam's best and brightest drilling skills into him that he wouldn't have acquired otherwise. Jace noticed that he had unconsciously lowered his respiration and heart rates like he was settling in for a long reconnaissance, and he knew without even looking that Gage had done the same thing. He had to give Holly credit, she held his gaze a long time—almost as if she was trying to find the door to his soul so she could waltz in and set it free. Mentally shaking his head he wondered where that thought had come from because he'd never been overly introspective. He understood enough about himself in his opinion so he'd never really seen any need to pry open doors that should remain nailed tightly closed.

Chapter 7

Holly had been only a couple of heartbeats from escaping when these two men had reminded her why opening her big mouth always seemed to get her in trouble. Damn it, if her mind hadn't been so flooded with those pesky endorphins, she might have been able to put a muzzle on her rambling. But oh no, she had to go and blab every single thing she'd been thinking like some freshman at a frat party. And the look on Jace's and Gage's faces had said it all…they hadn't been able to believe she'd read so much into what had happened. Well, Mother Theresa wasn't going to have a thing on her after tonight, because she wasn't ever having sex again…well, not for a couple of decades at least.

She felt like a balloon that somebody had just untied because she just slowly deflated. *I don't know how I manage it, but it seems to be a gift. Things are sailing along all sunshine and roses…and then I have to open my mouth and fuck everything up. Hell, I should write a play about my life. Who am I kidding? No one would ever believe it and when they called it a fantasy piece it would just piss me off. Might as well finish this off and answer their question because there isn't anything left to lose. Crap on a cracker, I'll be lucky if Aunt Daph lets me back in the office after these two get finished telling her what a loose cannon she has working for her.*

When she lifted her eyes to theirs she immediately realized two things. First, she had obviously been speaking out loud…again. And second, they were both about to stroke out. Time for damage control and fast. "I'm sorry. I can tell by your expressions that I was speaking out loud again…damn, I really have to get a handle on that before I hand over the keys to the kingdom." Realizing she'd just done it yet again, she slapped her hand against her forehead and sighed. "See, this is what I get for working alone for so many months on end. I start thinking and then to fill the silence surrounding me, I start talking." Giving herself a mental shake, she continued, "I was trying to get away because I could tell I'd said too much and I know guys don't really care about all that *touchy-feely* stuff and it was painfully obvious I'd made you uncomfortable…so it seemed prudent to leave." She knew she'd sagged against Jace when she'd finished, but she'd said it all without taking a breath because she had known if she ever stopped that she probably wouldn't have the courage to finish it.

Holly had always considered herself a direct person and she'd never tried to be anything but honest with anyone she was dealing with. It had never occurred to her that performing as multiple people was in essence lying until she'd found herself in the thick of it. The producers on Broadway were getting great plays, so they'd been happy. The directors she'd reluctantly worked on stage with had been thrilled with her acting, so it had been a wash as well. The only problem had been her parents, because they'd felt as if they'd been shortchanged when she had bowed out of their society functions at an early age. As soon as she'd "blossomed," as her mother liked to refer to her curvy figure, her parents had been on a single-minded campaign to get her whipped into what they considered "acceptable shape," *translate to twig-thin*, to accompany them to the many charity events and public functions their careers demanded they attend.

It had been Holly's great joy to move away from home at seventeen. She'd graduated from high school a year early and moved to college that same weekend. Since that first summer, she'd never lived under her parents' roof again. Oh, she'd been home to visit briefly during summer and semester breaks, but she'd always made sure those visits were brief.

Coming back to the moment, Holly realized they were studying her like they would an interesting exhibit at the zoo. Moaning she asked, "Did I say any of that out loud? Please tell me I didn't." The sheer humiliation of everything that had happened was finally taking a toll and she struggled to get to her feet once again. "Please, just let me go. I really have maxed out my humiliation quota and I'd appreciate it if you would let me just leave quietly." She knew her words had gotten so quiet that they had likely not heard everything she'd said, but at this point it didn't matter. All she cared about was making her way to the front door and then running as fast as she could in the hellacious heels she was wearing to the club's dock so she could take one of the small passenger boats back to Washington D.C.

* * * *

Gage had planned to let Jace finish this conversation with Holly because he knew the man had been battling a major hard-on for the woman for several months, but it was becoming all too clear that it was going to take both of them to keep up with her. He wasn't sure he'd ever met anyone whose mind functioned on so many different planes at the same time. How the girl kept her head above water was a mystery he wasn't sure he and Jace together would be able to unravel.

When he reached for her hand he felt her stiffen for just a second before she seemed to relax. "You've had the opportunity to say quite a lot, sweetness, and I have to tell you, that is not always going to be the case. Usually submissives aren't the ones doing the majority of the talking. But we don't know you that well yet, so we're taking this opportunity to remedy that some tonight. But—that being said, I want to make a couple of things very clear to you, so listen carefully." Gage had deliberately dropped the volume of his voice so that she would have to make a concentrated effort to hear his words and he'd also switched to what he'd heard the subs at Club Isola referred to as his *sex-as-sound* voice because he wanted her attention as well as her arousal.

"I'm sure that I speak for Master Jace as well as myself when I say, I didn't respond immediately to your answer because I was completely stunned by your insight and honesty. Your ability to use language to express your thoughts is remarkable and we were both surprised and pleased. But considering your various occupations, I don't suppose we should be surprised at all. Now, I'm going to tell *you* this, but I'll never cop to it if you tell anyone else, but I think we were both a bit speechless for a moment—something that doesn't happen to either of us very often, I assure you."

He'd seen a bit of light in her eyes and a faint whisper of a smile, so he knew his words had done exactly what he'd intended them to. He watched as Jace turned her face toward his own. "Pet, you are a remarkable woman and we're looking forward to spending time with you. We have a lot of questions about some of the things you said— hell, I need to find out some of those answers to figure out how the hell the fact that Daphne Craig is your aunt slipped through your background check." Gage was sure someone's ass was going to be on the hot-seat when Jace got wind of who had doctored Holly's file. He was guessing it had been Daphne herself, which meant any frustration the security team felt would evaporate into thin air. The older woman was a force to reckon with and had been with Ian since he'd taken over McGregor Holdings. If she'd considered hiring Holly important enough to go to those extremes, there was probably a lot to the story.

Jace stood up, keeping Holly cradled in his arms, and held her for just a few seconds before setting her gently on her feet. "Master Gage and I are going to escort you to the ladies locker room. There is always an attendant on duty who will be happy to help you with anything you might need." They'd started walking with her between them—making their way toward the main lounge. The music and voices coming from the party were getting louder with each step they took, so he knew the party was now in full-swing. At the door of the Ladies Lounge, as it was known, Jace turned her so that she faced them both. "Pet, when you come back out, one of us will be standing right here waiting for you. At that point, for tonight only, you'll be allowed to address us both by our first names while you are inside the club. We plan to teach you about the Lifestyle you are so obviously drawn to—but we'll do it as we go along. But tonight is a celebration for our friends and we want you to enjoy the party. Do not leave without speaking with one or both of us, are we clear on that point?"

"Um, yes, I guess so. But if it's like any other party and I didn't come here with either of you, why do I need your permission to leave?"

Jace watched as the independent career woman emerged right before his eyes and he smiled to himself, because this was the part he loved so much. Earning a submissive's respect wasn't that difficult when she understood that your own pleasure and satisfaction were a direct reflection of her own. But this thing with Holly was something altogether different, so he answered her accordingly, "Because the bottom line is, pet, we're both born and bred Texas boys, and our mamas would be after us with their wooden spoons if they knew we'd let the lady we were interested in take off in the night from a party all alone." He was pleased to see her relax a bit and the softness of her lush little body pressed against his chest as he pulled her into a hug that sent the last of the blood in his brain racing south. He needed a drink and he needed it quickly. As he turned her into Gage's waiting arms he nodded toward the bar and quickly walked away before he succumbed to the urge building inside him to take her right here against the wall. He knew that he needed to put a little distance between them or he was going to be balls deep in her soaking pussy again without any consideration to who was watching.

Chapter 8

Gage wanted to laugh out loud as he watched his friend stalk stiffly away. He was grateful he'd been left to see to Holly so he didn't have to suffer the same fate. His usual leathers helped keep a raging hard-on corralled, but the damned black jeans he was wearing for tonight's party wouldn't do anything to keep the oxygen-rich blood he needed to think straight from pooling around the head that didn't always make the best decisions.

Wrapping his arms around Holly, he leaned down and buried his face against the side of her neck and just inhaled her sweet scent. She smelled like an exotic flower—citrus-sweet and tropical—and a woman who'd just had a couple of off-the-charts orgasms. When he considered how responsive she'd been, he couldn't help but wonder what she was going to be like when he and Jace focused their considerable Dominant skills on her. Her submission was probably a bone-deep desire that someone had tried very hard to drive out of her by pushing her into a career she excelled at but that didn't fulfill that hole inside her that she didn't tell anyone about.

Gage's mom had explained it to him late one night several years ago when they'd been sitting on the back patio long after all the other members of their family had gone to bed. His mom had recognized him as a Dominant even before he'd known it himself. He'd always known that his mom took great joy in doing things for her family, but he'd also known that there had always been something deeper between them—and even though he'd known it was there, he hadn't been able to pinpoint exactly what it meant. Beth Hughes was no one's fool and it was her candid questions that night that had led to a discussion that had changed Gage's path.

He'd moved back to the ranch after leaving his SEAL team and despite working around the house, he hadn't ventured out much. The small town they lived near was gossip central and full of well-meaning mothers with marriage-minded daughters—all of those were complications he did not need. When his mom stated that she knew he was a Dom when he'd been in high school, he'd been shocked. He smiled at the memory of her bark of laughter at his surprise that night so long ago. But it had been more recently that Gage's mom had explained the difficult line career-minded submissives have to walk because their lives are usually starkly divided between their careers and their Master. Her detailed explanation of a sub's mindset and how difficult it was to fulfill both roles without a caring and compassionate Master who understood and listened, had been eye-opening. He'd benefitted from her insight several times, helping some of the extremely bright subs he'd scened with get to a place where they could step away from the armor they were forced to don each and every day just to survive in their workplaces.

Truthfully he'd probably used the information for many of the wrong reasons in the past, but in this moment—holding Holly in his arms, he knew exactly what his mom had been trying to tell him. He made a mental note to send her a big bouquet of her favorite wildflowers to let her know how much he appreciated her foresight. Pulling back, Gage brushed the silky dark waves of Holly's hair back from her face, and spoke, "Go on inside, sweetheart. I'll be right here for you when you're finished. But don't take too long. I've seen more than one Dom storm in there to retrieve his sub when he thought she was stalling." He smiled at her startled expression as he kissed the tip of her nose and turned her to the door.

Leaning back against the wall after she'd gone, he looked out over the party and smiled when he saw Callie. She was standing in front of Ian, his arms wrapped around her and resting over her lower abdomen in a protective gesture that Gage had seen many times back home. He and Jace had already started a pool on when they were going to make the announcement that she was pregnant, and from the look of the ever so slight pooch of her tummy, Gage didn't think they could keep it a secret much longer. Those close to the couple had noticed the subtle changes several weeks earlier. The fact that Ian was even more fiercely protective than ever had been the clincher. For just a split second his mind flashed to him holding Holly in a similar pose, they were in one of the local cantinas near their homes in Texas. In that second, he understood the joy of keeping that news to yourself, if even for just a short while. The intimacy of that shared joy binding the three of them together as nothing else ever could.

Jace's gruff voice roused him from his musings. "What has you smiling like the cat that snagged the canary?"

"Nothing much, just watching Ian and Callie. His body language gives away their secret to anyone who is paying attention, but at this point I think the joy on his face speaks even louder." Jace handed him a bottle of beer and he nodded his thanks while they both enjoyed the silence between themselves as they continued watching the celebration unfold in front of them. Gage finally decided it was time to get a couple of things cleared up before things went any further. "Listen, I don't know if she is *the one* we'd hoped to find someday, but I'd really like to find out. What is your plan?" When Jace didn't answer him right away, he added, "Are you planning to share her forever or will this be a deal like Ian's? Because I have to tell you, if I'm going to get cut out later, I need to know that up front."

Walking away from something that felt so right would be close to impossible, but being cut loose later would be even worse. Jace had kept his gaze on the guests milling around in the soft candlelight in front of them but his words went straight to Gage's soul. "She needs us both. I don't know how or why I know it—but I do. There is a hole in her soul and it's going to take both of us to help her heal. Hell, it's gonna take both of us just to keep up with her." Jace smiled and shook his head before his smile slipped away and he continued, "I'm gonna push her, I won't be easier on her because I'm so taken with her, and I don't want you to be anything but yourself with her either. Something tells me she has dealt with more than her share of phoniness, she doesn't need any more smoke and mirrors from us. There is heartache and loneliness in her eyes and I want to erase it as quickly as we can because she deserves so much more."

"I couldn't agree more. We'll have to work together and I'm going to depend on you to lead sometimes. I know you were raised in a polyamorous family, even if it wasn't public information, it was still obvious to anyone who cared enough to look closely. Since you grew up with an insider's view of what it takes to make it work, I'm asking you to help me do it right." Gage paused for several beats because he wanted to choose his words carefully. There was no way he would ever consider a sexual relationship with Jace, they were neither one wired that way. And he didn't want his friend to get that idea, but he wanted to be able to ask questions and benefit from Jace's background.

Before he'd figured out exactly what to say, Jace had picked it up and given him exactly the assurance he'd needed, "Let's look at this as a team effort. We both bring different skills to the table, or our woman's care in this case, but I'll lead when the situation warrants until you're comfortable in a fully equal role. Her head will probably fight us at every turn for a while, but I don't think her heart will be a problem. In the end it'll be worth it for all of us. Face it, you are going to learn this in a New York minute and we can always call Alex and Zach if we need another point of view."

Gage groaned thinking about how apparent it was that the two Doms he'd known when they were among the SEALS' best and brightest now spent their time trying to corral one tiny blonde package of dynamite. "Christ, you don't think Holly is going to be as difficult as Katarina Lamont, do you? Fuck, I may not be ready for this after all." They both enjoyed a chuckle as they looked over to see Alex pull his beautiful wife down onto his lap and whisper in her ear. And even though they couldn't hear his words, there wasn't any doubt about the topic of conversation because the flush that went over her cheeks as she lay her head back against his shoulder was a dead giveaway. Gage had to smile as they watched Alex, both of his hands clearly in view—one holding her dainty wrists together in her lap and the other cupping the side of her face in a tender move that was still laced with the message that he was her Dom and the moment was his to control. Watching as her chest began to rise and fall in what was obviously shallow, panting breaths, he knew she was close to reaching her release. Gage smiled as Alex deftly turned her face to his and sealed his lips over hers just as her entire body went rigid, and he knew Alex had caught her scream as he'd given her, what appeared to have been, a very satisfying orgasm right in the middle of room where one of the wealthiest men in the country was celebrating his marriage and collaring ceremony.

Seeing Alex end the kiss and wrap his arms around Kat as she buried her face in his shoulder almost felt as if he was eavesdropping on a private moment, but he was glad he'd continued watching. Seeing Alex cuddle Katarina for several seconds before sliding her over on to his brother's lap had been what their SEAL instructors had always referred to as a "teachable moment." The ease that the two brothers brought to their handling of their wife might look simple on the outside, but Gage was sure the three of them understood precisely where the boundaries lay. Suddenly he was filled with hope that the type of relationship he and Jace had talked about during all those late nights of endless reconnaissance might just be possible.

Chapter 9

Holly stood just inside the doorway of the ladies lounge as if she'd been frozen in place. She'd heard Katarina's name mentioned and that had caught her attention because she'd met Kat a while back and liked her immediately. And then she'd spotted Kat and Alex sitting just a few yards from the door and she'd been completely captivated watching as Alex Lamont made love to his wife. It didn't matter that they were in the middle of a wedding reception surrounded by a couple hundred of Ian and Callie's friends, nor did it matter that his touch had been perfectly acceptable for the situation…none of that had kept the man from giving his wife an orgasm she had obviously enjoyed very much. And he'd done it with nothing but his words…incredible.

Her mind was whirling with possibilities and suddenly an entire book seemed to write itself in her mind. These were the moments that she wished she could run to the nearest computer and spend the next several hours getting down the details she'd just watched play out in her imagination. Holly was pretty sure that had been the most erotic thing she'd ever seen and for once she wasn't really too worried about forgetting what she would normally be clamoring to commit to paper. Oh no, that scene was going to replay itself in her mind for the next fifty or sixty years. Each and every detail was etched in the granite of her mind. She wondered briefly if Kat would be willing to answer her questions…*God, that would be fantastic. I could get a firsthand account…I wonder if she would mind?*

Once Alex had settled his wife on his brother's lap, Holly saw him turn his gaze directly to her. She felt like a deer caught in the headlights of his intense gaze. A part of her knew she should look away, but there was something in his eyes that told her she'd be able to run, but never hide. The man was a Dominant to his very core. Working in Ian's executive offices meant she'd met both Alex and Zach Lamont on several occasions and each time she'd noted Alex's intensity. She knew Zach Lamont was a Dom also, but his demeanor seemed to be startlingly different. At first it had been a bit disconcerting because they were mirror image twins, but she'd quickly noticed differences in their personalities that made telling them apart easy...as long as they spoke or moved. Giving herself a mental slap she suddenly realized Alex's attention had caused both Jace and Gage to notice she'd been standing just behind them.

As Alex walked toward them she felt a wave of searing heat and the ice cold wash through her and for the life of her she didn't know what it meant. It was his posture and intent, but she didn't know why. Her fear must have shown on her face because she heard Alex's soft "What the hell?" And then there were black dots clouding her vision...and they were getting closer together...fast.

Holly could hear voices but they seemed so far away and suddenly she felt like she was floating, or maybe she was being carried, she really couldn't quite get her mind to function like she knew it was supposed to. When her vision cleared it was Zach Lamont's face, not Alex's that filled her view. She realized that he was taking her pulse and then oddly enough he leaned down and slipped her heels from her feet. Glancing up at the worried faces looking down at her, she groaned and turned her face into the shoulder of the man holding her. She instantly recognized Jace and she let herself relax into his hold, hoping when she opened her eyes again it would all have been just a bad dream.

* * * *

Jace had watched as Alex seemed to zero in on something behind where he and Gage stood, and just when he raised an eyebrow at the man in question he'd heard Alex shout, "What the hell? Catch her," and all his training had come back in the blink of an eye. He'd turned just in time to see Holly sway forward and her knees give way. He'd been a half a step closer, so he'd been the one to scoop her up just as she was falling limply to the floor. Now, holding her in his arms with her face pressed against his shoulder to hide her embarrassment, he felt as if all was right in his world, despite the evidence to the contrary. Alex was urging people back to the party with minimal luck and Jace nearly laughed out loud when Alex's five-foot-nothing "submissive" wife announced they were scaring Holly and everybody needed to move along. Jace wasn't sure which part he enjoyed the most, the fact that it worked or the stricken look on Alex's face.

He'd been relieved when Zach explained that he thought Holly had been standing with her knees locked for whatever reason and that had caused her to faint. Once Alex had settled Katarina in a chair alongside Callie, he and Ian both crouched in front of Holly. Gage was sitting right beside him with Holly's legs over his lap and when Alex explained that he'd seen Holly standing in the door watching as he'd "punished" Katarina for a flip answer she'd given him about whether or not she was enjoying herself, they'd all four laughed.

I have to give the man credit, he can improvise a punishment quicker than anyone I know. Alex had mentioned quite some time ago that he and Zach had been at their wit's end about how to punish Kat because she seemed to like everything they came up with. He'd laughed along with the other Doms at the table that night, but suddenly he had new respect for the men's dilemma. He and Jace were both pretty strict Doms, just as many of their friends had been. And one by one they seemed to fall, and as they fell in love with their women their interpretation of the BDSM rules and protocol seemed to shift. He'd worried about how that shift was going to play out in the club, but now he understood exactly why Ian hadn't been concerned.

"Pet, look up at us please." He'd kept his voice low hoping to keep her embarrassment at a minimum. He was satisfied when she raised her face and looked at each of the men surrounding her. "Feeling better, love? You'd have hit the floor if it hadn't been for Alex's attention."

"Oh yeah, Alex is the hero here. Geez, you guys are lame. Alex may have seen her eyes rolling back in her head like a china doll, but he's the reason she was standing there like a statue to begin with." Everyone, including Katarina Lamont, looked completely stunned by her remarks. Turning to Callie, she asked, "Oh shit, I said that out loud, didn't I?"

Callie burst out in a fit of giggles just as Alex growled, "Katarina, language. And you are in such trouble." He turned back to Holly and said, "We can't take her anywhere anymore." Jace was dumbfounded when the former SEAL winked at Holly, letting her know that he wasn't really mad at his outspoken wife. Holly quickly succumbed to the giggles when Callie didn't bother to hold back her amusement. And when Jace looked up at Kat she looked quite pleased with her results. The woman was quick thinking, he'd give her that. Katarina had obviously spoken aloud on purpose to break the tension of the moment and it had worked like a charm.

Everyone started to move away and give them a few minutes to get Holly settled. Jace and Gage both chuckled when they heard Alex speaking to his wife as he led her back to the party. "I know what you did—and why, love, but I'm still going to paddle your bare ass as soon as we're on that plane. We didn't soundproof that bedroom for no reason you know." Jace saw the little sub shiver and knew Alex was going to give her exactly what she loved.

Holly's quiet words brought his attention back where it belonged, "I think it's time for me to go. I'm fairly certain I have disrupted this party about all I dare if I want to keep my job. Good Lord, but this is so embarrassing. I've embarrassed you and myself...this is so out of character for me...really. I'm usually such a good girl."

Jace saw Gage stiffen next to him and knew Holly was in for it now. As long as Jace had known Gage, this had always been a major sticking point for him as a Dom. Anyone who decided they had the right to pass judgment about what constituted "proper sexual behavior" in Gage's presence would answer to him very quickly. Jace settled in for the verbal lashing he knew was coming.

* * * *

Gage's heart had nearly stopped when he'd turned and seen Holly on a fast track to the floor a few minutes ago. At Alex's words he and Jace had turned in what had to have looked like a well-rehearsed move toward her just as her knees buckled. Because Jace had been standing to his right, he'd reached Holly first, catching her in his arms just before she would have crashed to the rock floor. After Zach had checked her over, he'd assured them she was going to be fine and then he'd pointed out the heels Holly was wearing and shook his head. From what Zach had said, standing with her knees locked would have been bad enough, but with the fuck-me shoes she had on the problem had been greatly magnified. *So, sweetheart, you're going to be one of the subs at the club going barefoot. No more heels for you unless you are flat on your back and they are wrapped around one of your Masters' backs.*

He'd been lost in his thoughts of all the ways they could keep her feet from hitting the floor when he zeroed in on her reference to the fact she *usually* was such a good girl. It didn't take a team of NASA specialists to read between the lines that she didn't think her behavior tonight qualified as "good." Gage didn't have many *hot buttons*, but this was one of the biggest. Social constrictions governing what was perceived as "normal" had been created by somebody with a major stick up their ass in his opinion. And the guilt-trip tickets society handed out like they were a ride at a state fair were often attributed to religion. Hell, he'd read the Bible several times and had yet to see anything in it that clearly gave someone else the power to judge what happened between consenting adults.

He used his fingers to grasp her chin and lift her face so that their eyes met. "Sweetness, you want to run that 'good girl' comment by me again? Because what I heard was that you don't think you've been a good girl tonight, when by my estimation that is completely inaccurate." Gage saw Holly's green eyes widen at the growled tone of his voice, but he knew the minute his meaning had made its way through her sharp mind because her pupils dilated with arousal. *Well, well. It seems our little subbie likes a bit of a challenge. Let's see if we can push you just a bit farther, babe.*

Holly opened her mouth to speak and then Gage watched as a cloud of what appeared to be pure shame moved over her entire face. Christ, even her body language was suddenly screaming how remorseful she was. Her whispered apology was all she'd managed to get out before tears filled her eyes. "Tell me why you are sorry, Holly. I want to hear what you think you have done that you have to apologize for."

He could see she was trying to control her breathing, no doubt she was making a herculean effort to keep the tears from breaching her lower lids and streaming unchecked down her pink cheeks. Gage had been ready for any number of excuses, but he was completely surprised by her words. "I'm sorry because I've disappointed you." She couldn't possibly be serious. Blown away? Check. Intrigued? Check-check. But disappointed? Not even close. Holly seemed to pick up on his confusion and when he didn't respond she added, "I'm usually one of those people who *overachieves*, you know? I like to give one hundred and ten percent…always, that way people are pleased."

Gage studied her for several seconds and could feel Jace doing the same thing. When he finally spoke, his words were gentle but laced with steel. "I want you to listen very closely to what I'm about to tell you. Master Jace and I are both more than pleased with you. You are smart, responsive, and beautiful—and yes, I put those things in their order of importance." *That question flashed over your face like a neon sign, sweetheart.* "Now, until we can sort this all out, I have a request." Gage saw Jace's nod so he was sure his friend knew exactly where this was going. "Master Jace and I would like for you to avoid whoever it is that has brainwashed you into believing you have to be perfect all the time. We'll be happy to run interference for you until we can be sure you're ready to face that person and tackle their condemnation alone." He saw her eyes go wide and knew he'd nailed it.

Jace spoke up as well, "Don't look so shocked, pet. We've both been Doms for a long time and we listen closely to what subs say and even closer to what they don't say. And you, love, are a classic case overachiever. You said earlier you are interested in exploring our lifestyle, is that still the case?" His wait for her response wasn't long, because she immediately nodded her head. He stroked his fingers down the side of her face before cradling her soft cheek in his palm. Gage knew Jace was using touch to center her attention and he was pleased to see how well it was working. Jace waited a few seconds before continuing, "We won't ask you any more about this right now because I know it's been a very long day for you. And I don't think our command is an unreasonable one. We are just asking you to avoid whoever it is that demands your perfection until we have a chance to help you work through some of those issues, because I have to tell you, your insecurity is unfounded."

Gage took her hand in his and was surprised to feel how cold it was. "Christ, sweetheart, your hand is freezing. Are you cold or is there something else we need to know about?" When he checked her other hand it was warm, so his curiosity was more that piqued.

"No, I'm not really cold." She let out a shuddering breath and then gave them both a wan smile, "I think I must have twisted a bit when I passed out because my back is hurting a little. Nothing serious, just some little electrical shocks here and there. Usually if one hand is cold and the other is warm, that means I'm due a trip to my chiropractor or masseuse."

Gage wanted to growl his frustration, but he kept his response in check. Despite the fact that this was exactly the sort of thing a sub should tell her Dom immediately, Holly wasn't a trained or experienced submissive. She was a successful career woman who was obviously well-versed in taking care of herself. "Sweetheart, from this point forward, this type of thing is going to be considered important information for you to relay to either Master Jace or myself immediately."

"Why on earth would you want to know about my little aches and pains? Goodness, you're too busy for that sort of thing. And I've always managed pretty well in my opinion, so I'm certain I can continue that without burdening either of you." And there it was, some of that spirit that he'd known was buried under all that sweetness. Gage didn't know about Jace, but he certainly hadn't expected to see it surface so soon, but he was sure pleased with the opportunity to address this issue right out of the gate.

"Well, sweetheart, that is where you are wrong, because of your agreement to find out where your interest in BDSM leads, you have given over care of this lovely body to Master Jace and myself. A very large part of our training of your mind involves caring for your body as well, so it is imperative that we know when things hurt, tingle, are numb, etc. Your safety and well-being are, and will always be, our chief concern. And while you are in our care, we'll take that responsibility very seriously. So, do you think you can avoid whoever has been selling you a bill of goods for a few weeks and keep us in the loop about your health concerns?"

* * * *

Holly knew she wasn't due to see her parents for at least a month, so avoiding them and their friends ought to be a piece of cake. Seeing nothing to lose by her compliance, she agreed. They helped her slip back into her heels with an admonishment to not wear them for extended periods of time again, and then walked alongside her as they moved back to the McGregor's party. The party was in full swing and appeared to be a resounding success. The music was lively, but playing quietly enough that it didn't impede conversations. Holly found herself relaxing and enjoying the conversations around her and relishing the fact that either Jace or Gage was touching her at all times. Just that small gesture made her feel special and it was a feeling she was sure she could get used to in a hurry.

Finishing her second glass of wine, Holly was starting to regret skipping breakfast and well, now that she thought about it she hadn't taken time to eat anything all day. When she tried to study the monstrous clock that hung over the bar to see exactly how long it had been since she last ate anything substantial, she frowned because the damned thing looked like it was underwater. *What the hell?* Just as she was about to ask what was wrong with the clock, she heard a voice that made her blood run cold.

Chapter 10

"Wyatt darling, get your Mistress another drink before I ask Master Ian to break out the St. Andrew's cross so I can give you a few lashes. Ignoring me is not in your best interest, you know." Holly would have recognized the screechy voice of Madeline Holmes anywhere. Hell, the witch had been her mother's best friend for as long as Holly could remember. Even though the voice was all too familiar, the words she spoke sounded totally foreign coming out of the mouth of a woman who was the epitome of stick-up-the-ass snooty prim and proper.

Madeline Holmes was a regular on every social page in the city. Holly had often referred to both Madeline and her own mother as one of the "wicked wonders" of New York society. Both women's parties were among the most highly coveted invitations in the city and their inner circle was tight and filled with only those considered to be of equal social standing. The idea that Madeline and her husband were attending a party in a BDSM club was enough to make Holly's head swim. Gage was the closest to her and he had evidently picked up on the change in her because he leaned down and spoke against her ear, "What's wrong, sweetheart? And don't you dare try to lie to me."

"Could you step directly behind me please?" Holly knew her request might sound odd, but she wanted to be shielded from Madeline's view if possible. She was relieved when he didn't question her, but smoothly moved so that he was standing behind her. He wrapped his arms around her and leaned back down, kissing her temple before sliding his lips down to her ear. Anyone watching would have only seen a man romancing a woman, not a woman hiding from the only woman who could guarantee Holly would have to break the promise she'd just made to Gage and Jace. Because if Madeline saw her, she would unleash the hounds of hell in the form of Celeste Mills-Forsthye, her mother.

"Sweetness, as much as I relish this position, the tension is coming off you in waves and I want to know who or what has caused it. Talk to me."

She took a deep breath and let it out slowly hoping it would calm her panic enough that her answers would make sense. "I promised you I would stay away from the person who always tells me I'm not good enough and that's my mother." She was sure they could have probably guessed as much, but at least now it was *out there.*

"Are you trying to tell me that your mother is here?" Gage's question reflected his surprise, and she nearly laughed at the absurdity of her mother ever being caught in a BDSM club. But then again, Holly would have told you the Pope would become a Southern Baptist before Madeline Holmes would be in a sex club also, so what did she know?

Holly tried to contain the hysterical giggle that threatened to surface and she felt Gage's arms tighten around her. "No...not my mother, but her best friend. Her voice is...um, well, distinctive is the most polite way to put it. Madeline Holmes is my mother's best friend and if she sees me here, word will reach my mother at the speed of light, I assure you." She knew she had spoken all the words without so much as a single pause, but she was truly rattled to her core. Not only was she in a sex club, she had been drinking in public, was in the company of *two* men, and had heard Madeline's words to her sweet husband. Each of those things would be a strike against her and she could feel herself sinking like the Titanic.

"Mistress Madeline is a friend of your mother? Seriously? She is one bad-ass Domme. I wouldn't have figured her for the best-friend type. Interesting." Gage's voice didn't do anything to hide his amusement, but for some reason it didn't calm her at all. He'd obviously noted she was still holding herself completely rigid in his embrace, because he pressed butterfly kisses over that sensitive place just below her ear and then whispered, "I'm sorry, sweetness. I wasn't trying to make light of your problem—you surprised me though, hell, I'd have never seen this one coming."

By this time Holly felt Jace's presence by her side and looked up and saw the concern in his expression. As Gage quickly explained the problem, Holly saw Jace's eyes scan the room. When she saw his gaze pause, she knew he'd found the Holmeses. "She speaks of you being here and Ian will see to it that she is banned from every club on the eastern seaboard—but that doesn't fix your problem, pet, so, let's get you out of here until we can sort this out."

Jace and Gage stepped back at the same time and since Gage was still holding her, she was forced to step back quickly or fall unceremoniously on her ass...*again.* Of course that was the exact moment the alcohol decided to course through her system like the swollen rivers she'd rafted during her last trip to the mountains. Her head started to spin and she stumbled giving away the fact she was struggling to keep up.

"Shit. We're going to have a serious discussion about your footwear, sweetness." Gage's words should have sounded harsh, but they didn't. She felt him steady her and Jace flanked her, his much larger body essentially blocking anyone's view of her as they casually walked from the large room. Once they'd reached a door she hadn't even noticed, Jace keyed in a code and the door swung open and they moved through quickly. As the door latched closed behind them, Holly heard the lock engage and nearly sagged as relief swept through her. Gage picked her up and made his way down the brightly lit hallway.

Even though she had visited Club Isola several times in the past few weeks on work related trips, she'd never been further than Ian's opulent office which was just inside the front entrance. She'd only seen the main room once and that was at nine o'clock in the morning, so its only occupants had been the cleaning crew. She was quickly coming to realize just how little she actually knew about Club Isola.

The corridor they were moving through was wide and lined with ornately carved wooden doors each with a security keypad. She wondered what all of those doors could be hiding, but her curiosity was quickly put aside when they stopped in front of a door at the very end of the hall and this time it was Jace who tapped in the code. The lighting in the hall had been subdued but not dim, and the stone floor was polished to a brilliant sheen. There were lovely landscape paintings on the walls, and nothing about the passageway reflected the nature of the club.

Holly couldn't have been more surprised at the beautiful apartment they stepped into. The entire space looked as if it had copied down to the last detail from *Architectural Digest*. "Holy shit!" The minute the words left her mouth she regretted her outburst. "Oh, crap, I'm sorry. That was terribly rude, I know, but wow…this place is beautiful."

Gage's one word reply of thanks left her speechless as he set her gently on her feet and immediately leaned down and slipped her out of her shoes. She sighed with relief and wiggled her bare toes in the plush rug. She wasn't sure whether she was feeling off kilter because of the wine or because she'd been carried yet again, but she took time getting her bearings before she moved around the room. She took in the beautiful décor noting the ivory and rich browns that were highlighted by dusty blues. The furniture was masculine, but not overtly so. It was obviously designed for someone much taller than she was, but then that took in most of the population over the age of twelve.

Realizing she was rocking back and forth from her heels to the balls of her feet—a move she'd always done when she was nervous and distracted—she suddenly stopped and looked up to find both men watching her intently, amused expressions on their faces. Deciding that silence probably wasn't her friend in this instance, she asked, "Who lives here? Or is this just like a hotel suite or something?"

"Jace and I share this apartment, although until tonight he had been spending most of his time at Ian's." She could see the humor in his eyes and that helped put her at ease. But it turned out to be the calm before the storm. His next words sent her on a quick mental scramble searching for an acceptable way to answer honestly. "What have you eaten today, Holly?" Giving herself a mental head slap for getting so caught up in the preparations that she hadn't taken time to eat anything, she sighed with resignation. *Just as well spit it out and take the tongue lashing that's sure to follow. Geez, why do people get so bent out of shape if your dietary habits don't meet their expectation of acceptable. Baffling, I tell you.*

Jace cupped her chin with his big hand and smiled down at her, "Not really all that baffling if you think about what I explained to you earlier this evening. Your physical and emotional well-being are our chief concern and our responsibility. But you were right, best to just answer honestly and endure the tongue lashing." She could tell he was trying hard to hold in his laughter at her unease, and strange as it was, that relaxed her. *Heck, how bad can it be if he's still willing to tease me?*

"Well, I didn't exactly eat anything today. I was just thinking about that earlier, before I heard Hagatha, because I couldn't figure out why the wine was kicking my ass and I'd only had two small glasses…well, that and the clock thing. But in my defense, I was busy working until the ceremony started and then you…" she waved her hand between them, "well, you *distracted me* and damn…on a good day I might have been able to twist this around until it was your fault somehow, but I'm just too tired to make the effort to be perfectly honest with you."

"Well, much as I do not condone your poor eating habits, I do understand that you had a busy day. But, it's time to get something nutritious in that empty belly of yours so hopefully you'll be awake long enough to carry on the conversation we're planning to have with you later. But for now, I want you to lay back on this sofa and rest for a few minutes while we fix us all a snack." Gage led her over to a sofa that must have been nine feet long and four feet deep. *Good God, who besides the Jolly Green Giant needs a sofa this big?* But the minute she lay back and snuggled into the most comfortable piece of furniture she'd ever laid on, she decided its size was a nonissue because it was like stretching out on a giant cloud. The pillow he'd placed under her head smelled faintly of the cologne she recognized as Gage's scent and the soft throw he placed over her was enough to make her wish she could just sleep the night away in that very spot. The last thing she remembered was him kissing her on the forehead and saying they would be back before she knew it.

* * * *

Gage leaned his head back and laughed out loud for the first time in ages when Holly told them that she didn't have the energy to twist things around so they were responsible for her not eating all day. He'd been livid at first, but his frustration had dissipated quickly as she'd continued speaking—more to herself than to anyone else. God Almighty, the little bit of a woman had curled up on their sofa and was sound asleep before he'd even left the room and she was absolutely perfect for them. She was honest, hard-working, and whip-smart. And it seemed to him that her irreverent sense of humor was probably something she only fully revealed after she'd gotten to know someone fairly well. Hell, when they took her to Texas to meet their families they might have a battle on their hands when they wanted to bring her back with them.

Walking into the kitchen, Gage wasn't surprised to see Jace already chopping vegetables for omelets. They'd discovered years ago that they both liked a big breakfast and it didn't matter to either of them what time of day it was served. Falling into their usual routine of teamwork, Gage let the silence between them settle like a comfortable fog on a warm summer night.

After several minutes, Jace broke the quiet, "She's amazing. Hell, even I'm surprised at how incredible she is and I've been watching her for months." Gage heard his friend let out a sigh and just waited. He'd known Jace Garrett forever and he knew the man wasn't finished. "Tell me what you think of the mess with that bitch Madeline Holmes. How that vile bitch slipped through our security checks still chaps my ass, but without a solid reason to ban her, we're stuck with her and her weasel of a husband."

"Well, for what it's worth, I think Holly is in the best position to tell us how much of a threat she is to her. I wish you could have been there when she heard the woman's shrieking voice—hell every muscle in her little body went on alert. And when I asked her what was wrong and she asked me to step behind her, I knew we had a serious problem." While it would be common for a submissive to make that kind of a request of her Master or a Dom she'd scened with numerous times, it was a request for protection and that implied a level of trust he was pleased they'd obviously already developed. Apparently having worked together a couple of times coordinating events had set the stage for tonight and he was grateful for that, because she'd certainly needed their help to get out of the room without being seen.

"Christ, I was about burst out laughing when she called the old bat Hagatha. Fucking perfect." Jace didn't even try to contain his laughter and Gage understood exactly what he meant. Madeline Holmes was a piece of work by anyone's standard. She'd browbeat every sub and many of the Doms with her rich-bitch attitude and arrogance. Ian had been about to pull his hair out over how to get rid of her and was pissed as hell when the two of them had shown up tonight. Oddly enough it had been Callie who had convinced Ian that sending them back to the hotel they usually stay in while in D.C. was going to be more trouble than it was worth despite the fact she'd been about eight shades of ugly to Ian's sweet sub at every opportunity.

"I'm anxious to hear Holly's story, but I'm not sure it's going to happen tonight. She was out like a light before I even left the living room. I think we need to try and get some food in her and then take her to bed. I don't want her trying to get back to the city when she's this tired, her guard would be down and she wouldn't be safe." Gage grimaced to himself—he always prided himself on being honest with others as well as himself, but Holy Mother of God, that was about as lame-assed as it came.

Jace stopped chopping and looked over at him and laughed, "Jesus, that was pathetic, you wanna try that again, cowboy?" *Shit, I am never going to live this one down.*

Chapter 11

Jace had heard some lame excuses in his time, but Gage's attempt to justify keeping Holly with them overnight was surely going to rank as an all-star favorite. Christ, the man didn't have to make excuses at all in Jace's opinion. Just saying, "I want to hold her all night" would be all the reason either of them should need.

When they had things mostly set up for a quick dinner, they both went in to wake Holly. Jace was a bit worried when they first started trying to rouse her because she seemed completely unresponsive. Since sleeping light often saved the lives of soldiers, neither he nor Gage would ever be accused of sleeping soundly. Jace had been known to come completely awake if Callie so much as sighed when she'd slept between Ian and himself.

Jace had actually been relieved when her pretty green eyes fluttered open. Her half-lidded, sleepy confusion was adorable. He could tell the minute she realized they'd been trying to wake her and why she was in their apartment to begin with, because her brightly flushed cheeks were a dead giveaway. They sat her up slowly, letting her get her bearings before leading her into the kitchen. Once they'd settled her at the table they began piling food on her plate and he saw her eyes widen in alarm. "What's wrong, pet? Don't you like breakfast?"

She blinked her eyes a couple of times before answering, "I love breakfast. And this looks wonderful, but I can't eat this much food this late at night. Good grief, I'll get even heavier and God knows what kind of nasty-grams that would bring my way. Lord in heaven, I shudder to think. And let's face it, I just don't have the muscle mass you guys have to burn this many calories."

He and Gage both froze and looked at her, not believing she'd actually had the nerve to say that after they'd just spoken to her about her self-deprecating comments earlier. Gage leveled his gaze and Jace could see he was struggling to maintain his calm as he cautioned, "Sweetness, I'm going to give you one chance to rephrase that before I upend you and warm up your sweet ass so you'll remember the lesson a bit longer next time."

Jace wanted to laugh out loud when he saw Holly's eyes go wide with surprise and then immediately her pupils dilated and he could see her pulse pick up at the base of her graceful neck. Her breathing hitched and her small gasp was the stuff of wet dreams. *Oh sweet Holly, each of those responses are tells that no Dom worth his salt would miss. You are more than a little intrigued by that spanking idea.*

"Oh…well, I'm sorry, but this is just a lot of food, and um, I don't eat late at night. Crap-o-molie, someone would probably send my mother a memo and I'd be getting e-mails, texts, and phone calls by dawn." She'd spoken the last sentence so quietly he'd barely made it out. Jace hadn't even met her mother and he already disliked the woman. And since he'd heard her rambling earlier about Daphne being her aunt, he couldn't help but wonder which of her parents had grown up with Ian's ultra-organized assistant. Because Daphne Craig was a lot of things, smart, outspoken, dedicated, and fiercely loyal among them. But he'd never seen her be judgmental or cruel, so it was easy to see why she was sheltering Holly.

"Pet, eat your dinner and then we have several things we need to discuss before this goes any further." He saw the disappointment in her eyes just before she lowered them to her plate. Looking up at Gage, he knew his friend was as puzzled by her reaction as he was. "Holly, look at me." When she slowly raised her eyes he saw her unshed tears. "Tell me what I said that made you sad, because I'm not sure you understood what I meant."

"No, it's alright. I appreciate the dinner, really I do. But I'm not really very hungry now. I think I'll just get my shoes and make my way down to the dock so I can catch the last ferry back to the city." She was already pushing her chair back and starting to stand before she'd even stopped speaking.

"Sit your ass down and eat your dinner—*Now*." Jace was getting mighty tired of this dance and knew the growl in his voice had no doubt made that crystal clear to her. Shit, had anyone ever spoken nicely to this woman? She had obviously been so browbeaten by someone that she assumed everything anyone said to her was negative.

Even though she didn't look particularly pleased, she sat immediately and started eating. She must have enjoyed the food because she'd completely cleaned her plate before he or Gage had finished. He wanted to tease her, but knew from experience with his younger sister, Abby, that would be a sure-fire way to ensure she wouldn't eat for the next couple of days. He'd no more than set down his fork than Holly was on her feet and quickly clearing the dishes. Watching her was a study in contrasts—her movements were so efficient it was almost as if they had been practiced in advance, but there was no denying how nervous and unsettled she was. He knew she was trying to delay their talk and he was determined to give her a few minutes to settle herself, but what he wouldn't give to know what was whirling through her mind.

When she had finally put away, cleaned, and scrubbed away every available excuse to avoid the inevitable, she turned to them and sighed in resignation. Jace had to bite the insides of his cheeks to keep from laughing and Gage's cough next to him did little to cover his own laughter. "Do you always clean when you are stressed, pet?" He didn't need to hear her words, the answer was plainly written all over her face. Hell, he would wager her apartment was nearly sterile.

"Yes. It's an odd habit, I know. But cleaning everything around me helps me clean the sludge from my mind as well." He knew her answer was a baseline honest response and he appreciated her insight as well as her clever turn of phrase.

"Come here." Jace stood and held out his hand to her and was pleased when she had started to step forward even before his words could have registered. Seeing her respond so quickly to his outstretched hand was a major *tell* about the depth of her submission, and one he knew Gage would have noticed as well.

Moving into their large living room, he settled her in a straight-backed chair, making sure she was facing them both. He wanted her comfortable enough to answer questions, but not so relaxed she forgot the importance of this conversation. "Let's start with a few basics, shall we? First of all, from the comments you've made this evening, Gage and I are both aware that your job at McGregor Holdings isn't what you usually do." When he saw her eyes widen in realization, he smiled, "Oh indeed, you do speak your thoughts aloud and I can't tell you how much that fact pleases us."

"Sweetheart, we would like to know exactly what you were doing before you became your aunt's assistant." Gage's words had been a direct inquiry as well as a declaration of a fact Jace was sure she hadn't realized she'd shared. *Well done, my friend.*

Holly blinked at them several times before she rolled her eyes—a move that ordinarily got a sub pulled over his lap in a heartbeat, but in this instance, he was fairly certain her disgust was with herself. "Oh brother, I really have to learn to contain that yakking out loud thing, don't I? Geez, it's hard telling what all I've spilled. I'm just a regular Chatty Cathy, fricking fracking...oh shit, I'm doing it again." He watched in amusement as she let out a dramatic sigh before continuing, "Okay, here's the short condensed version. I'm a screenwriter. Well, I've written plays also, but you get the idea. I have also written several novels. And well, I've done a bit of acting. That was a kind of an accident though. Anyway...each of those requires me to be a different person and it got to be overwhelming and when I knew I was just one more sleepless night from being ready for the rubber room, I came down to see my aunt.

"The day I walked into McGregor Holdings there wasn't anyone at the front desk so I made my way down the hall to Human Resources and asked to see Daphne Craig. They were swamped and misunderstood who I was. They thought I was some girl from the secretarial pool and told me my job as Ms. Craig's assistant started right now, rather than the next week. Well, I thought it was a joke when they directed me to Aunt Daffy's office, so I took the paperwork up with me."

When Holly glanced between them she knew they weren't going to say anything until she'd finished, so she'd continued. "Well, you know my aunt...she's a steamroller. She took one look at the paperwork and rather than the laughter I'd expected, her eyes lit up and...well, she started rattling on about this being proof that God loved her and a scathingly brilliant idea if she'd ever had one...and I guess the rest is history."

Jace was totally bewildered at how this woman had slipped so easily through their security system. *Christ what kind of holes have I got to close up? I can't fucking believe this.* "Care to enlighten me as to how you managed to slip through our security checks?" He tried to keep the frustration from his voice because it really wasn't her fault, but he and Daphne Craig were going to have a come to Jesus meeting of the first order next week.

Holly flinched and looked up at him, her apology written all over her face. "I'm really sorry about that. But that one is all on my sweet aunt. And evidently the girl who was supposed to have the job was Holly Miller, so it wasn't that much of a stretch." She paused for several seconds, suddenly very interested in her tightly clenched fingers resting in her lap.

"And?" He knew there was more, it was written all over her body language and they needed to get this all sorted out before anything else happened between them.

"When Ian didn't recognize me, we decided I'd help her get things organized and caught up in the office because she and I have always worked well together...much to my mother's disdain. And I used my real name instead of one of my pen names or other aliases so of course your clearance report came back clean as a whistle." She looked up at him and he could see how worried she was about the problems she and her aunt had caused.

"Well, that is still no excuse for my staff's oversight. A clearance that comes back perfectly clean is almost always phony or has been purged, they should have flagged it immediately. And what the hell is going on in H.R. anyway? Christ, Ian should have been having a damned heart attack, especially since all of this took place during that fiasco with Callie."

"See, that was the thing. It just sort of got out of hand and then I think Aunt Daffy was hoping I'd stay because she could see I was recovering just as she'd hoped I would." Holly had dropped her gaze to her hands again as they twisted the fabric of her dress until he was sure the wrinkles would never come out.

Gage leaned forward with his elbows resting on his knees and shook his head, exasperation clearly racing through him. "Well, the way I see it we need to be thanking our lucky stars that the problems with our security clearances and identification of employees has been pointed out to us this way rather than through a tragedy." Waving a hand in Jace's direction when he'd started to speak, he continued, "No, hear me out. I agree, we are going to have to overhaul the system. We have people in positions that they are clearly not qualified for or they are just completely fucking up, so they'll have to go. And I want to hear Daphne's explanation as well, because she understands the importance of security as well as any of us. But most of all, I want you to explain what you meant by recovering."

Jace had heard Holly's words, but they hadn't really registered because he'd been so pissed about the fact his security team had dropped the ball in such a big way. This is exactly why it would take the two of them working together to keep up with Holly Mills. Shit, he didn't have any idea how long it would have taken him to get around to asking about that statement.

"Oh shoot. I thought maybe you were going to let that go by. Fuck a duck in a rainstorm, should have known that wasn't going to happen with two Doms. Are you two always going to tag-team our conversations? Because I have to tell you, this is going to be damned inconvenient for me if you are."

Jace nearly laughed at the growl he heard come from Gage. "Pet, that is one. You have already agreed to be ours while you explore the lifestyle and the attraction between us. And you have already been told to answer questions immediately and honestly. So that little dance of deception you just did in a very futile effort to avoid answering Master Gage's question just cost you a punishment later this evening. Now, if I were you, I'd answer that question before you rack up another."

He'd heard her small gasp of surprise and then watched as her face flushed a beautiful shade of rose. Her nipples poked through the soft fabric of her halter dress and he watched as she shifted in her seat. *Trying to relieve some of that pressure on your needy clit, baby?* Her responsiveness was amazing and he couldn't wait to finish this so they could fuck her seven ways to Sunday.

"Well, you see...I wasn't kidding about skating on the edge of a physical and emotional collapse...that is why I'd come down to see my Aunt. Aunt Daffy has always been my rock. Even when I was a kid, I'd figure out ways to get sent to her house over holidays. Everything was always so normal at her house and it was healing. I had been burning the candle at both ends for several years before I got here. And, I have still been working on a few projects during the evenings, but..." She chuckled and looked up at them and smiled.

"Well, my dear sweet aunt had your IT guys install some kind of timer on my laptop, damned thing goes off at nine o'clock each night and won't turn back on until the next evening at six on weekdays. Aunt Daphne was determined that I would get the rest she'd decided I needed to bounce back. And as much as it chapped me in the beginning, I *have* gotten a lot of rest and am finally feeling my creative side starting to reemerge. So you see, she had her reasons for keeping quiet even though I really do understand your frustration and I'm sorry for my part in it." She took a deep breath and then seemed to pull energy he knew she wasn't feeling right out of thin air as she stood up. "Well, I'm going to head back now. I'm sure you are tired and I'd like to get back to my motel before it gets too crazy. It's hard to get through the lobby sometimes."

"Sit down, Holly. You weren't given permission to get up let alone leave. We aren't finished with this discussion yet, not by a long shot. And why is it hard to get through the lobby?" Jace was getting more frustrated with this discussion by the minute, was there ever going to be an end to the crap they were finding out about their so-called team of security experts? Hell, now they had an employee whose permanent address was a damned hotel? Seriously?

"Oh well, sometimes there are people there that recognize me and if it's late and they're drunk, they want me to join them for…whatever. Even though some of them only know me because of my parents and that is just too disgusting to even think about." She looked up and flushed, "I'm sorry, that was probably one of those *too much information* things, wasn't it?"

"No, pet, there will never be any *TMI things* when it comes to you. We not only want to know everything, we'll demand it. Now, we'll finish sorting this out on Monday, quite frankly, I'm too pissed to work it through right now and I've got other ideas for you tonight."

Chapter 12

Holly had been convinced Jace and Gage were going to both have strokes when she'd started explaining how she'd come to work for Ian without them realizing who she was. She'd been shadowed by security teams her entire life so she was well aware of how anal they were about any *breach* of their system. But she was also well versed in ways you could bypass them if you played your cards just right. Hell, her mother's family was *old money* and it chapped their asses that Daphne worked when she clearly didn't need the money. Holly knew her aunt's career had been all about rebellion in the beginning, but from what she understood, once Ian had taken over for his father, she'd wanted to stay and help the young man become a success.

But it was Holly's father's fame that had always been the greatest cause for concern. Robert Forsthye was one of the biggest actors in Hollywood, even though he'd never actually lived there. His salary for films was obscene and his public exposure was a constant challenge for Holly. Groaning to herself, she wondered how long she'd be able to hide her connection to him. It was obvious that Jace and Gage weren't big movie magazine readers or they probably would have pieced it together by now. Holly didn't relish that discussion either. Holy hell, if they were the protective or jealous types her life and social circle were going to drive them away quickly. Resigning herself to enjoying what little time she would have with them, she decided to just learn what she could about the BDSM lifestyle because so far everything she'd read and seen had sparked her interest in a way that nothing had in a very long time. She'd already been thinking about ideas for a book and heaven knew she could use all the firsthand experience she could get because her previous sexual experience had been dismal to say the least.

It shouldn't have surprised her that the men who had claimed to be interested in her had always been interested in her mother's family connections or her father's fame or their collective portfolios. She'd learned early on that she was just too plain to capture the interest of any man that she found interesting. And her mother had nearly come apart at the seams the first few times Holly had expressed an interest in one of the *bad boys* at her school.

When she finally returned her focus to the two men sitting as still as statues watching her, she was relieved when she realized for once she hadn't been thinking aloud. "Pet, your mind is so loud you didn't even hear Master Gage and I speaking to you. We'll be able to help you silence the noise in your head so that you can enjoy a respite from the pressure you put yourself under at every possible turn. We'll help you learn to let go, but I want to warn you up front, we're going to take our responsibilities seriously. There are going to be a lot of times when we restrict your activities for your own sake, and you'll likely be pissed as hell about it. Just remember, your safety and well-being are *always* our main concern. It's our privilege and right to care for you."

Jace had been right when he'd mentioned her mind being too loud for her to enjoy living in the moment. She had always been plagued by attention deficit disorder symptoms and had learned to control the worst of the symptoms by keeping several balls in the air most of the time. Jace didn't know it, but his promise to help her get outside of herself…even if it was for a short time…was a temptation she'd never walk away from willingly. She didn't doubt that all the baggage that went along with being Robert Forsthye's daughter would quickly become overwhelming and that wasn't even considering the unnecessary drama of dealing with her mother.

Resigned to the reality that this relationship would burn out as quickly as the fireworks she saw dancing over New York harbor every July fourth, she quickly refocused her thoughts on how much she enjoyed those fireworks despite how quickly they faded. She always stood on the small terrace of her penthouse and watched as the bright colors lit up the Statue of Liberty. The entire city seemed to pause for those few minutes to watch as the night sky was filled with flashes and explosions marking our nation's birth. She now realized how sad she was when the show was over…as if she was missing something and hoped the feeling of emptiness wasn't a preview of coming attractions.

Turning her attention back to the men sitting in front of her, she noticed their frowns and wondered what she'd done to merit such fierce expressions from them both. She wasn't sure what could have gone wrong so quickly, but in her experience, being direct was the best path when someone was angry and you hadn't gotten the memo explaining all the particulars. "Care to enlighten me about why you are both frowning at me? Or should I check my email for a memo? Hell, at least my mother sends a memo." She knew her laugh had done little to lighten their mood but then, she hadn't really been kidding either. Hell, Holly had started getting memos in the form of bulleted lists of her transgressions and *suggestions for improvement* before she'd gotten out of grade school. She had to give Celeste Mills-Forsthye credit, she knew how to cut someone down to size with words more efficiently than anyone else Holly had ever encountered.

Both men's expressions had changed from frustration to disbelief and Gage's question reflected his dismay at her statement. "Your mother sends you memos telling you why she's pissed off at you? Are you fucking kidding me?"

"Yes and no…in that order. Geez, I'm a writer and even I'm not creative enough to make up something *that* insane. Her memos are usually bulleted lists. And if I don't respond to her texts, emails and faxes, she has been known to send them by courier. Oh indeed, mama-Celeste does not take being ignored well at all." This time her laugh was more genuine because the looks on their faces were beyond priceless. When they didn't appear to be on board with her amusement, she added, "I'm sorry, but you really shouldn't judge her based on your experiences with Aunt Daffy, because they are polar opposites I assure you."

Both men shook their heads as if they were having a lot of trouble wrapping their imaginations around *all things Holly*. She was starting to regret having shared so much because it would probably just lead to her being rejected sooner. *Someday you're going to learn to keep your big mouth shut…obviously not today…but someday.*

* * * *

Jace knew it was time to begin Holly's training because she'd managed to leave them once again. If he and Gage didn't get a handle on her mental meandering quickly, they were going to lose credibility as Doms and that was the fastest way Jace knew to sink the entire relationship. With a quick nod to Gage to make sure he was ready, Jace used every bit of focus he had left to be sure his voice reflected the change in direction of their conversation. "Stand up."

Watching as Holly snapped back to the moment, he saw her blink quickly. Jace knew she probably thought they were sending her away—she'd find out soon enough that wasn't the case at all. He watched as resignation flooded her expression and when she stood up from the chair she immediately turned and started to take a step toward the door. "Stop! You were only told to stand up, pet, not to walk away. And by the way, you never want to walk or run away from your Dom—not ever." He watched her closely for any signs of fear and was thrilled to see nothing but anticipation tinged with unease. A bit of discomfort was fine because it would help focus her attention, but he didn't want her to ever be truly afraid of either of them. "Since this is just beginning for you, I want you to understand that during a scene, you'll address us as Master Gage, Master Jace, or

Sir. Failure to use the proper address will be corrected quickly. We know you'll make mistakes and the punishments will increase as time goes along."

Noting that she was standing stone still with her eyes flitting between them, Jace decided to push her a bit. Crossing his arms over his chest, he tilted his head just a bit to the side and gave the one word command he knew was going to be her first make-or-break moment, "Strip."

Jace wanted to laugh out loud when her face flushed a deep red and she looked at Gage, the unspoken question in her eyes. He knew she was trying to decide if they were serious, but to her credit she didn't say a word. Deciding he would give her five seconds to begin before addressing her noncompliance, Jace leaned forward ever so slightly. He had to hold back his smile because her eyes went impossibly wide at the move. *Oh you aren't going to miss a thing are you, pet?*

She surprised him by refocusing her attention on him and slowly moved her shaking fingers to the side of her dress and slid the hidden zipper down her right hip. Then, raising her hands to the back of her neck, she unhooked the back of the halter and held the dress against her breasts for a couple of seconds before dramatically letting the entire garment slide to the floor. It felt like all the blood in his body was pooling in his cock and he had to fight the urge to shift in his seat. She was standing in front of them in nothing but the tiniest bit of lavender lace he'd ever seen anyone refer to as underwear. Her nipples peaked tighter under his stare and he let her pause for a few seconds before raising a brow at her. His silent question was answered when she moved her hands purposefully to the top of her panties and hooked her thumbs under the elastic before sliding them down her thighs. Once they hit the floor she bent at the waist and picked up both pieces, folding them, she placed them carefully on the chair behind her.

Jace swirled his finger in the air, the silent instruction to turn around was clear and he saw her hesitate. "Now, Holly." He'd seen that same pause in subs before and it always mystified him that they didn't mind a Dom looking at their bare breasts, but ask them to turn around so you could see their ass and they balked. Every sub he'd ever asked about it had given him the same answer, patiently explaining that women always consider their asses to be too large. Jace watched as she pulled her bottom lip between her teeth and bit it in a move that made her look exactly like the innocent that he'd bet a week's salary she was. She began turning and he wanted to laugh as she quickly brought herself back so she was facing forward.

Gage had moved so that he was standing beside Jace's chair with his arms crossed over his chest. Jace could see his reflection in one of the mirrors they had placed strategically around the room and knew his pose would be intimidating to Holly. "Move your feet a bit over shoulder width apart. A little further, that's fine. Now straighten and lengthen your spine. Perfect. Put your hands together at the small of your back and grasp your wrists. When we tell you to assume the standing pose, this is what we'll expect you to do." He saw her tense and knew exactly what she was thinking, so he answered her unasked question, "Yes, naked. For now, we'll want you naked as much as possible so you become accustomed to how it feels to have the air wafting over your exposed skin. It will also help you learn to become more attuned to your own body. Careful, pet. I can read that look. You may not believe me now, but I assure you, I'm right." He didn't bother to tell her that she would quickly get over her unease at having others see her lovely body because she was going to be spending a lot of time in various stages of undress in front of others.

Chapter 13

Gage stepped forward and pressed his palm gently against the small of her back and watched as her muscles immediately started to relax at the touch. Holly was clearly a very tactile sub and that would serve her well because both he and Jace were firm believers in the power of touch in Ds relationships. "Your body responds to my touch and that pleases me, sweetness. Keep your eyes on Master Jace. Let him see the fire that burns within you. Show him how much you desire what is ours to give you." Gage heard Jace's growl and almost laughed because he could well imagine the view his friend was getting from their little fire-ball.

He deliberately rotated his palm so that it cupped the perfect globe of her ass letting the tips of his fingers skim over the tight puckered ring surrounding her rear hole. "Has this sweet ass ever been fucked?"

Gage heard her soft gasp even though it had been so quiet he wasn't sure Jace would have heard it. He knew in an instant that she hadn't, but he needed to hear her speak the words. "No, well, not really." Her voice was so light—the sound reminded him of the bits of white cotton that filled the summer breeze back home and just the picture of that brought a smile to his face.

"Not really? You want to explain exactly what that means? Because I was thinking it was actually a basic yes or no question, so I'm having trouble processing that *not really* part of your answer." Oh he knew exactly what she meant or at least he thought he did, but a big part of what they'd be teaching her was going to be the need for her to be totally transparent with them. Considering how she'd been in the past, he expected it to be one of her bigger challenges.

When she didn't answer him right away he gave her ass a quick swat—not enough to really hurt, but enough to get her attention and sting a bit. "Oh...oh my, that was...that feels like...a slow burning ember that wants to become a spark but isn't quite enough. Oh fraggle you asked me a question, didn't you? Shit...don't tell me, I've got this one..." Gage looked up at Jace and knew from the smile tugging at the corners of his lips that he was as captivated by Holly as he was. Holy hell, if he didn't know better, he'd swear she and Callie were sisters.

Gage stepped up behind her and pressed his bulging cock up against her bare ass so she'd know what she was doing to him. He leaned down and spoke into her hair, "Baby, as fun as it is listening to you, I really am going to insist that you answer the question. Let me help you out her a bit—I asked you what not really meant."

He could almost hear the wheels pick up speed as they whirled in her mind. "Oh, well, in college, well, *oh, merde, c'est le bordel.*"

Gage looked up at Jace and grinned. *Oh baby, you are toast if you think you can curse in French to avoid punishment.* "Sweetheart, that's two and this is not a mess. It's a simple question and one I'm getting more and more determined to hear the answer to the longer you stall."

"Two?"

"Submissives are not allowed to curse, so that pretty sounding French word that means shit that you tried to slide by? Well, that's one." He chuckled when he heard her murmuring under her breath. He caught just enough to figure out she planned to switch to Italian and that wasn't going to work out well for her either.

"*Figlio di puttana.*" Even though she'd just called him a son of a bitch in Italian, there hadn't been any heat in her words and he was fairly certain she was testing the waters more than commenting on his mother's personality.

"That's two. And sweetness, my mama isn't gonna take kindly to you saying she wasn't married when she had me, just so you know." Gage hadn't even tried to keep the amusement out of his voice.

Jace was sitting in front of them shaking his head and chuckling. "Holly, you're going to rack up a lot of swats this way. Master Gage is fluent in several languages and knows how to curse like the sailor he was in several more. It's in your best interest to just answer his question, because I've already added to his count for your delay."

"Well, crap on a cracker, I don't even like to think about Lyle Thomas, let alone confess to being naked with him. And admitting that he shoved the base of a lit candle up my ass and then told me I had to suck him off before it burned me is pretty humiliating. And then finding out his friends had been watching...well, that's why I left college and never looked back." Gage was seeing red—literally—by the time she'd finished speaking. Jace was on his feet in a blink and had pressed himself against Holly's front as tightly as Gage was pressed against her back. He wrapped his large hands around her wrists and pulled them apart, unlacing her fingers from where they were still clasped behind her back. Gage moved her arms slowly so the blood flow didn't return too quickly and send needles of pain down her arms.

As far as Gage was concerned, life as Lyle Thomas knew it was over. He found himself taking deep breaths to keep the anger from bubbling to the surface and scalding the one person who least needed to witness it. There was definitely a long run on the beach and probably a round or two in the gym's boxing ring with some unsuspecting fool in his very near future.

* * * *

Jace wasn't sure Holly's words had been completely finished when he'd already been moving to stand in front of her. He'd seen the stark devastation in her eyes and God he was proud of her courage.

She'd followed Gage's command and never broken her gaze from his own, even though it had been clear just how much it had cost her. Jace knew Gage well enough to know that he was holding in his anger by the barest of margins and neither of them wanted Holly exposed to that right now, so they'd just tag-team and Jace would step up and lead for a few minutes until Gage could rein himself in.

Pulling back from her so he could look into her sweet face, Jace was shocked at what he found. Where there had been heat and desire a few minutes ago, now there was nothing. Her eyes were practically vacant and the complete lack of emotion stunned him. If the incident had been recent, he would have assumed she was in shock, but by her own account it had happened a long time ago. The only other explanation was that she hadn't ever told anyone until tonight. That realization tore through his mind like a wildfire and all he wanted to do was make love to her until her eyes were once again filled with passion.

Smoothing his thumbs over her cheeks in soothing strokes he spoke softly, "Pet, I want you to know both Master Gage and I are humbled and honored that you trusted us with your story. That's not to say we aren't mad as hell at the man who hurt you, because we are. But our anger is directed at him and it doesn't change the way we feel about you, except to make us admire you even more knowing what you've been through. And knowing your interest in this lifestyle survived that incident speaks volumes about just how much you must feel like you have been missing something when it came to relationships and sex. Does that sound about right?"

Jace didn't doubt for a minute that he was right, but he wanted to draw the point to Holly's attention. He was relieved to see her blink a few times as if she was trying to bring the world back into focus and then her eyes locked on his and she nodded. "How did you know? I have never understood why…I mean, why would I still want this? But I've always felt like a there was something out there that everyone else knew…some celestial secret that made relationships and sex meaningful, and that I'd missed the memo. Kind of like reading a self-help book that has a few of the middle chapters missing. I know I'm not explaining it very well, but…well, maybe you know what I mean or you wouldn't have asked, right? Because that sounded like a rhetorical question now that I think about it."

God almighty the woman didn't miss a trick. Jace briefly wondered what her IQ was, he was willing to bet it was well into the gifted range because even as shell-shocked as she'd been, she had managed to sort it all through in just a few seconds – remarkable. "Your capacity to understand yourself and the people around you is going to be a wonderful blessing to you as you learn to embrace your submissive nature. You're going to find that missing piece, I promise you." He leaned down and kissed her on the forehead, enjoying the feel of her soft, warm skin pressed against his lips. The sweet scent of her wrapped around him and suddenly the energy between them seemed to crackle with desire.

When Holly turned between them so that she could see both of their faces she lifted her small hand up to cup their cheeks in such a sweet gesture Jace turned and kissed her palm. "You are both very nice men and I'm very lucky you have offered to help me. Thank you for listening. I have never shared that story with anyone because I feared the judgment I was so sure I'd see in a man's eyes." As much as Jace wanted to argue with her, he kept his silence and was grateful when Gage did the same. "But you didn't judge me and I want you to know that I'm grateful."

Jace found himself so caught up in the emotion of the moment that for several seconds he couldn't manage to speak around the lump that filled his throat. Gage looked as overcome as he felt but his friend had found the words when they had escaped Jace. "Sweetheart, you are a gift straight from God." Jace watched as the smile he'd seen Gage use on women so many times swept over his face like a slow-moving tide. "But none of this changes the fact that Master Jace and I are both going to paddle your sweet ass. I do believe you have three punishments coming and at about four swats each, you've managed to rack up a pretty healthy spanking, baby."

Smiling as he saw Holly's green eyes deepen to a rich shade of emerald green in just a few blinks, Jace watched as Gage showed their lovely sub the punishment pose they preferred. Standing back looking at her smooth ass all ripe and ready for their hands was enough to make any Dom smile. They let her fidget for a few long minutes, knowing the anticipation would be a punishment in itself. They wouldn't always allow her to hold on to the edge of a table or chair, but for this first spanking, they didn't want her to be surprised and go ass over teakettle.

Stepping up behind her, Jace rubbed her ass cheeks while he spoke to her, "Since you owe me four strokes and I don't usually swat as hard as Master Gage, I'll be warming you up so you are ready for his eight. We are perfectly capable of counting so we won't demand you do it, but you are not allowed to come unless you are given permission." He was squeezing her flesh so that the blood moved to the surface so she'd be better prepared and then he'd run his fingers down between her beautiful thighs to find her pussy soaking wet. *Perfect.* "Pet, you are very wet. This just may not be the punishment you are anticipating after all, I'm wondering if you aren't going to enjoy this just a bit." He and Gage shared a silent chuckle when her entire body shivered in anticipation.

Jace made sure his first strike was a slightly cupped blow that generated more noise than fire. He heard her gasp of surprise each time his palm landed against her delicate skin, and when he delivered the last one she had let a small moan escape. Stepping up closer he fingered her pussy and didn't even try to hide his smile from Gage. "Oh, baby, you are so wet." He slid two fingers deep inside her and pumped several times until he felt her internal muscles beginning to flutter. "Oh no you don't, pet. No orgasm for you just yet, you'll need to learn patience because my love, your releases are Master Gage's and mine to give."

Stepping back, Jace watched as Gage moved up and ran his long fingers between her legs. Jace knew by the way her entire body seemed to tense that Gage was circling her clit. Gage quickly withdrew his hand no doubt just a few seconds before she would have come because Jace saw the muscles in her legs tremble just as she moaned in frustration. Gage delivered four hard swats with his palm flat, landing each blow in a slightly different spot and alternating sides. Holly's ass was a nice bright pink already, so they'd need to watch her closely for signs of bruising because Jace knew Gage's last four strokes were going to be doozies because he was not likely to cut her any slack for calling him a son of a bitch.

"Stand up, Holly." Jace was surprised to see that she'd been crying because he hadn't heard a sound from her during her paddling. Gage's voice was stern and Holly had responded to his tone immediately. When she weaved a bit as the blood left her head, Jace watched Gage steady her with a hand to her elbow. Once he was sure she was ready to stand on her own, Gage stepped back and began unbuckling his belt. Jace knew Gage wasn't going to use it on her, but obviously she didn't. Panic filled her expression and Jace wasn't at all surprised to hear the sob that bubbled up from deep in her throat—what did surprise him was seeing her turn on her heel and sprint for the door.

Chapter 14

Holly had barely gotten her bearings after both men had given her four swats. Cripes her ass felt like it was on fire and then when she saw Gage unbuckling his belt she panicked. Her mind flashed back to the headmaster at her private school and the one and only time she'd been punished at school. The man had insisted she'd been the one he'd seen taking cookies from a tray despite her repeated denials. She'd tried to explain that she didn't even like peanut butter so she sure wouldn't steal peanut butter cookies. But he'd been insistent and the lashing she'd gotten had left her with welts and bruises that had required medical attention.

There was a part of her mind that was aware running was futile, but she was drowning in blind panic and the fear won out over reason. Just as she reached the door she felt a hand clasp around her upper arm just as the headmaster had grabbed her. A brilliant white flash of fear went through her mind a second before everything went black.

* * * *

"*Fuck.*" Gage knew the instant he'd touched his belt it had been a mistake. Every bit of color drained from Holly's face and her expression was absolute stark terror. He hadn't planned to give her the last four lashes with the belt, even though calling your Dom a bastard was really a very serious offense. He had been planning to strip and knew Jace was preparing to do the same. But because he hadn't told her that he wasn't planning to use it on her, he'd be lucky if she would ever be able to trust him again. He never wanted to see that expression on her face again and damned well not when he was the one she was terrified of.

When she'd turned to run, he'd watched her hurdle the coffee table and sprint full out for the door. He'd barely managed to catch her before she opened their front door and the minute he'd wrapped his hand around her arm to stop her he'd felt her freeze and then she dropped like a stone. *What the fuck?* Even with his hand clamped around her arm he hadn't managed to keep her head from snapping forward. Gage was certain if he lived to be a hundred he would never forget the cracking sound of her head hitting the heavy oak door or the sick feeling that rolled through him as he watched her terrified eyes roll back just as the lids closed. Seeing her long, curled lashes resting on her pale cheek nearly made his heart stop beating.

"She's hurt—call the bar and get Zach Lamont up here and see if any of the club members who are medical professionals are still here." Gage could see that Jace was already dialing his phone before he'd even finished speaking. Without listening to any of the conversation taking place, Gage settled Holly on the sofa before running to his bedroom for a shirt to cover her. He'd just managed to cover her and was buttoning the last button when the room flooded with people.

Zach Lamont was the first through the door and Gage was relieved to see he had a med-bag in hand. Zach's time as his SEAL team's medic had given him a lot of experience with a wide range of injuries and the fact that he was also a Dom would make explaining what had happened much easier. Zach lifted Holly's eyelids and flicked a small penlight over each pupil and frowned. "How long has she been out?"

Glancing at his watch, Gage answered, "Just shy of two minutes." Gage knelt next to Zach so their words wouldn't be heard by everyone in the room. *Why are there so fucking many people in here? Jesus, somebody clear the damned room.*

Gage nearly choked when he immediately heard a booming voice ordering all "non-essentials" out of the room. When he recognized the voice of Mitch Grayson he understood why it had seemed as if someone had read his mind. Mitch was one of the most gifted empaths around, the man's ability to "read" another person's feelings and often their thoughts had saved his SEAL team more times than any of them would ever fess up to. Gage had heard stories about it for years and he knew Mitch had recently helped Callie as well. Looking up at Mitch, Gage merely nodded his thanks before turning back to Zach.

"Talk to me." Gage appreciated Zach's curt statement while he continued with his examination because it didn't matter which group of Special Forces you worked in, they all understood the importance of clear, concise communication between team members. Just as he was finishing giving Zach a rundown of the events leading up to Holly's injury, her eyelids started to flutter open.

* * * *

Holly felt like she was slowly floating to the top in a bowl of Jell-O…and that wasn't counting the fact that she was sure someone had hit her in the head with a two-by-four. *Holy shit I have a headache.* Once her eyes started to open she could see there were people standing around her but there wasn't anyone here that she knew. *Oh holy shit, you've really done it this time Holly. You really better get out of here. Who are these people and why does my head feel like it's going to explode?*

Trying to sit up, she realized someone had their hand firmly on her thigh, her very bare thigh. Glancing down she realized two things, one…she wasn't wearing much at all and two…what she was wearing obviously didn't belong to her. *Oh fuck, I've really done it now. What kind of party is this and what did they give me? Think…what's the last thing I remember? I left class…walked to the student union to get lunch…no that's not right. I went to see Aunt Daffy…why did I do that? Shit, my head hurts too bad to think.*

"Please, I need to sit up."

Holly had spoken the words without even realizing it until one of the men kneeling in front of her said, "No sweetheart, you stay right where you are. Let Zach check you out. You've been hurt and we need to know that you are alright." She blinked up at him, but didn't remember ever having seen him before. Why did part of her feel like she should obey this man? He was really cute in a surfer meets bad boy sort of a way, but he looked like he was already out of college so she wondered why he was at a frat party. *Oh shit…that's where I was…the party…oh, God…no!*

* * * *

Mitch Grayson had been standing beside the sofa listening to Holly, trying to get as much information as possible before stepping in, but the minute she started to thrash about in a blind panic he spoke up. Looking at Zach, he asked, "Is it safe to sedate her?"

Zach shrugged, "I don't feel good about it because I don't really know the extent of her injuries. I don't see any overt problems, but I can't really be sure." Zach and Gage were struggling to help Gage hold the little tiger still, but she was obviously terrified.

Alex Lamont stepped up to the end of the sofa and spoke in a voice that caused everyone in the room to freeze. "Holly. Stop. Now."

To no one's surprise the woman stilled instantly, blinking up at him in confusion. "Who are you? What makes you the boss of me? And aren't you a little old to be at a frat party?"

Mitch wanted to laugh out loud at the expression on Alex Lamont's face, hell, this one might have just broken Kat's record for shocking the man no one on his team had ever seen speechless before Katarina reentered his life. It seemed to take Alex a couple seconds to push back his surprise before his entire face seemed to light up from his smile. Mitch just shook his head, damn the man could switch gears in a heartbeat and turn on the Lamont charm with his next breath.

"My name is Alex, Holly. And you are right, I am too old to be at a frat party. Now be a good girl and stop fighting the men trying to help you, alright? I promise we'll get you exactly where you need to be as soon as possible, deal? Oh and would you feel better if I brought in some reinforcements for you?" Alex looked over the tops of several people until Mitch knew he'd spotted Kat and Rissa at the back of the room. Motioning them forward, both Alex and Zach's wife and his own wife scrambled closer.

Pulling Rissa close he whispered in her ear, "Baby, she doesn't remember anything that happened tonight, nor does she remember Jace or Gage and that is going to kill them. She thinks she's at a frat party and something bad happened there so tread carefully. We're setting up to fly her to the hospital, but Ian won't let Jace fly because he's too upset, so he's bringing someone over to do it. She's going to balk at going to the hospital so we'll need your help with that one." He bit her earlobe and smiled at the catch in her breathing. "Don't block me, baby. I can feel you trying and it's just going to delay that hot sex you're craving."

Rissa shuddered and then he felt her mind open, "That's a good girl. Now help Holly and then come to the hospital with Bryant. I'm going to fly over because I can hear her and I think I can help." She nodded and moved closer to Kat who had been watching them closely. Katarina Lamont was no one's fool. Mitch didn't doubt for a minute she would let Rissa lead because Kat knew Mitch had given her vital information.

Mitch smiled as Rissa leaned toward Holly and started chattering like they were old friends, which for all Holly knew at this point, they were. "Hey, girlfriend, you look a little worse for wear. I think we should see a doc about that goose egg on your noggin. Damn, girl that looks like it hurts. I heard those hot guys over there talking about a helicopter ride for you, oh you are one lucky sister."

True to form, Katarina Lamont didn't miss a beat, "Are you shitting me? You're going to ride in a helicopter? Damn, I think maybe I need to kiss the concrete, too. And with hot guys, too...you go girl. We'll have to drive there, but we'll be probably be there by the time you get out of ER. You want us to smuggle you in anything?"

Holly was blinking at them as if they were insane, but slowly nodded, "Yes, I'd really love to have an Almond Joy. That is if it's not too much trouble. It's kind of my comfort food of choice."

Gage was lifting her in his arms as Kat waved her hand as if dismissing the comment, "We know that...Almond Joy it is. See you soon...and I am so getting all the details later on the hot guys." Mitch was impressed that both women had played their college pal roles to perfection, but then again, maybe he should be more worried than proud. Giving himself a mental head-slap, he turned and quickly kissed Rissa goodbye before making sure she was safely in Bryant's arms. Sharing Rissa with his best friend Bryant Davis was the best thing that had ever happened to Mitch. He'd wanted her for so long, but had waited until Bryant returned from a year-long job in Japan before he'd really pushed the issue. And there wasn't one single thing about his life he'd change.

Chapter 15

Holly was about to go stir-crazy trapped in the damned hospital room, well room wasn't really a very accurate description of the "room" she'd been given. Between her parents' barrage of phone calls to the hospital's administration, her aunt's micromanagement, and Ian's intimidating presence, she'd been spent the last several days lounging around in a suite that rivaled the Hilton. After she had been poked, prodded, and scanned within an inch of her life they had moved her into a beautiful "prison" and told to *rest* which was the most ridiculous thing she'd ever heard. Who could get any rest in a place where there was a perpetual parade of people in and out all day and night? And the two hotties that seemed to have taken up residence were more than just a little distracting as well.

She'd learned from her friends Kat and Rissa that their names were Jace and Gage, and evidently she'd just been starting a relationship with them when she'd been hurt. Both women had assured her that she was perfectly safe with them, but it had been Ian McGregor's endorsement that had carried the most weight. Holly had known Ian since she'd been a kid and he'd always treated her with respect and she knew he was honest to a fault. It wasn't that she didn't trust her Aunt Daphne, it was just that she knew her aunt had a vested interest in seeing Holly "taken care of," her words, not Holly's.

Daphne had always believed Holly needed someone in her life to help her navigate troubled waters. Her aunt had assured Holly she wasn't being critical, just practical. She'd told Holly she wouldn't be around to be her guardian angel forever, and if she had to be replaced it might as well be with a hot man.

Really, there was nothing wrong with her, well except the fact she still had huge holes in her memory. But the doctors had assured her it was just a matter of time before everything came back so she didn't see any reason she shouldn't be allowed to go back to her small apartment at the edge of campus. It wasn't the Ritz, but at least it was quieter there and she could start on her first novel...*oh, wait. They said I already did that...shit, I hate not being able to remember things.* Sighing, she had just swung her feet over the edge of the bed when Gage and Jace both stalked into the room.

"Where do you think you're going, pet?" Jace was always calling her that and she didn't really understand why, but it didn't sound like he meant it to be degrading so she'd let it go. *Crap, I'll bet they have this room under surveillance. Hell they probably know everything, yeah nothing humiliating about that.*

"I'm tired of being cooped up here. I am fine and I'm going home today. They can't keep me here against my will. That has to be kidnapping or unlawful restraint or *something*. I can't get any sleep here, there are people in and out all the time. And some crazy guy was here this morning yelling about a play he wanted me to finish. I need to get back to my apartment and see if I can figure out what the hell he was talking about. Where's my purse? I'll need a credit card to get a plane ticket. And where are my real clothes? I'm tired of these damned yoga pants. Shit, I don't even have any shoes. And the girls said I should be getting really great sex, and well, I'm not getting that either, so why stay?" She suddenly realized that she had been pacing the width of the room and that the floor was suddenly tilting to one side and all of the sudden she was so hot and dizzy. *Damn and double damn as Kat would say, why do I have to do this with these two here?*

* * * *

Jace had known if they just waited Holly out, she'd tire quickly and then they could tell her that she was in fact being discharged in just a few minutes, but she wasn't heading to New York. No, the ass-hat that had managed to charm his way past the nurse had shown them she could expect more of the same if she returned to her penthouse in the Big Apple. He and Jace had spent the last couple of hours setting everything up and the girls would be arriving momentarily with clothing and personal products from Holly's motel room. They'd already had everything else boxed and moved to the storage in the basement of McGregor Holdings.

Both men would be forever grateful to Katarina and Rissa for all their help. Their ability to convince Holly they'd been friends for years had been remarkable and all four of their husbands had wondered how often those same skills had been used on them. "You will have clothes *and shoes* as soon as Kat and Rissa arrive, but you probably won't need them since you're going to be too tired to walk." He smiled when she flopped back onto the bed in exhaustion. Holly's doctors had warned them that adequate rest would speed her healing and consequently the return of her memory. They had also emphasized distracting Holly with something other than her usual activities. Their reasoning had been that there would be a lot more pressure to "remember" if she was back at work or in familiar places.

Jace and Gage both planned to see to it that their little sub got plenty of rest and relaxation. Their families had been updated and would help as needed, but the three of them would be staying in the small guest house behind main house on the Garrett's ranch. Abby was home for a few weeks after some kind of problem at one of the drill sites and Jace was more than a little anxious to find out what that was all about.

Kalen Black and Logan Douglas were also tagging along for some much needed R & R. Neither of the men had taken any time off in the three years they had worked on Ian's security team. They added staff after Callie was attacked and now that those men were fully trained it was time for them to take some time off and blow off some steam. Smiling to himself, he remembered the last time all four of them invaded his parents' ranch. They'd nearly eaten his mom out of house and home, and driven Abby insane with their teasing. Hopefully things wouldn't be as chaotic this time.

"You know, I'm really getting tired of being tired. How much longer is this crap going to last because I have finals in just a couple of weeks. I wonder where I left my books? Oh, I'll bet Rissa and Kat will bring them with my clothes. Do you think they'll bring my laptop, I'm sure I need that. Or did I leave it in New York? God damned goose in a G-string…not being able to remember sucks I tell you." Holly had closed her eyes and within seconds he could tell she was fast asleep.

Jace looked at Gage who was shaking with silent laughter, "Christ she's entertaining. I swear though, sometimes it's exhausting just listening to her mind race all over the place." Gage walked over and covered Holly with a soft throw her aunt had brought the first day she'd been hospitalized.

The minute the soft cashmere touched her she sat up and blinked at him. "Oh, hello. When did you guys get here? I guess I fell asleep. When am I getting out of here? Oh wait, I was leaving wasn't I? But I'm waiting for something…oh well, maybe it'll come back to me while I get dressed." Shaking his head, Jace watched as the entire scene played itself out again, almost word for word and step for step as Holly paced the room. The doctor's biggest concern had been the fact that not only had Holly's long term memory been randomly affected, her short-term memory seemed to stutter from time to time as well.

Kat and Rissa both breezed in the door and proceeded to take over. They tried to get all the men out of the suite, but none of them were even close to falling for that one. "Well, crap on a cracker, we never get to have any fun. Texas isn't that far from Colorado, you know…you could come up and visit. Hell—Oh.…" Kat's shoulders slumped and she looked over at Alex and Zach ruefully.

"That's one, kitten. Alex warned you in the elevator. I'm beginning to wonder if Holly's memory problem is contagious." The sting of Zach's promised punishment was cooled considerably by his smile, but Jace didn't doubt for a minute she'd be getting the promised punishment. He had heard both Kat's husbands fuming about their inability to get their sweet sub to stop cursing no matter how creative they'd gotten with the punishments.

"Well, shoot." Kat's shrug told Jace that she wasn't overly concerned and he smiled at the frown on Alex's face. Turning back to Holly, she explained with her typical enthusiasm, "If it's too cold to have a girls' party by the waterfall, we can always use Layla's beach room. Oh sister, you should see what her men built for her, it's fu...um...fundamentally awesome." Every Dom in the room—except Alex was either outright laughing or battling it for all they were worth.

"Katarina, points for creativity, but a punishment for intent. Now, be good subs and get Holly ready for transport." Kat nodded and turned away from him before rolling her eyes. "I know you rolled your eyes at me Katarina, and that's one more." Jace smiled because it looked like Kat was finally starting to worry a bit about what was coming her way.

"Transport? What am I a sack of potatoes? Really?" She leaned closer to Kat and whispered, "Really Kat, he seems a bit...well, I'm not sure exactly how to describe him." Holly seemed as if she was genuinely concerned for her friend and that warmed his heart.

Rissa piped up, "Stern...there's a word for you. Accurate, but not profane or disrespectful." She smiled and looked over at Bryant Davis who stood with his arms crossed over his chest. His indulgent smile belied the fact that he was usually second only to Alex when it came to being a stickler for protocol.

"Well said, love." Bryant's praise seemed to light Rissa from the inside out. Jace knew the three of them were anxious to get home to their daughter, Betsy. From all accounts, the little girl was as gifted as Mitch and a carbon copy of her redheaded mama.

Holly looked between the two women and then laughed, "Well, Rissa's gonna get laid because she spouted off some PCBS and Kat's getting punished by the guy with the stick up his ass because she isn't politically correct enough with her B.S." Both Kat and Rissa went instantly still and Jace heard their gasps. But it was the shocked look on Alex Lamont's face that was Jace's undoing. For the first time since Holly had been hurt, Jace felt the weight that had been pressing down on his chest lift as he tilted his head back and roared out his laughter.

Chapter 16

Their flight to Dallas-Fort Worth had been uneventful. Holly had been asleep before they'd gotten out of the hospital's parking lot, and she'd barely stirred when he'd carried her onto Ian's private jet. Gage had gotten her up before they landed so she could freshen up and eat a snack before they hit the road to the ranch. It was a two-hour drive without a lot of options for convenience breaks and he and Jace both knew better than to show up at the Garretts' if they'd already eaten. Good God Jace's mom could cook up a storm, and his mouth was already watering just thinking about all the things she'd have prepared for them.

Walking Holly down the steps of the jet, he was relieved to see their rentals had been delivered right on the tarmac. *Oh yeah, ya gotta love Daphne Craig.* Gage and Jace had spoken with Daphne the day after Holly had been hurt. Her story was identical to Holly's except she was much more forthcoming about how close to the edge Holly had been when she'd arrived in D.C. Daphne told them that she had originally seen the opportunity as a way to keep Holly close so she could monitor her health and well-being, but as time went on and Holly seemed to be doing fine, it had become increasingly obvious she'd made a huge error by doctoring the H.R. documents and security clearance.

Daphne had already confessed to Ian by the time he and Jace had cornered her. To her credit, she had offered Ian her resignation which he'd graciously declined. There was still some tension between Daphne and Jace, but Gage felt confident their friendship would be stronger in the end. Gage hoped that was the case, after all, she was Holly's aunt and family was family.

Mitch had taken them aside at the hospital and explained how truly confused Holly was. She understood that she'd been hurt, but couldn't remember how it had happened. Hell, she thought she was back in college, which meant she was missing several years of her life. They had spent a lot of time with Holly the past few days reviewing where their relationship had been when she was hurt as well as where it had been headed. Gage had been more relieved than he wanted to admit when he'd seen the same spark of interest in her pretty green eyes that he'd seen that first night. The fact that she was still interested in finding out about the lifestyle spoke volumes about the depth of her submissive personality.

Settling her between them in the backseat of the black Expedition, Gage was happy to let Logan Douglas fold himself behind the wheel. The man had a photographic memory, which had certainly come in handy since his specialty with the teams was explosives. The man just seemed to love blowing up shit, whether it was sanctioned by Uncle Sam or not—thus his nickname Boomer. Logan had been in a very dark place when he'd first retired. It hadn't seemed like any amount of bullying or beer had made a dent in his melancholy until Callie had entered Ian's life. Hell, who was he kidding? The woman Ian called *Carlin* had pranced right in and taken over all of their hearts.

Callie would always hold a special place in the hearts of all the security team. It had been her quick thinking that had taken down a corrupt U.S. Senator, his evil wife, and put a stop to the political aspirations of their son. Just thinking about that bastard and what he'd done to Callie as a teenager was enough to send Gage into a flash of anger. *Just five minutes alone with the fucker, that's all I'd need, and four and a half of those minutes will be spent fighting my way to the front of the line.*

Refocusing his attention on the sweetheart seated next to him, Gage noticed the tension seemed to be coming off her in waves.

Pulling her small hand into his, he was shocked to feel how cold it was and he didn't miss the fact that it was trembling as well. "What's wrong, sweetness?" When she didn't seem to even realize he'd spoken to her, he put his finger under her chin and turned her face to his, "Holly? I asked you a question and I expect you to answer me. What's wrong?"

"Oh, I'm sorry. I was just kind of lost in thought I guess. Well, I just realized that I'm going to a place where I don't know anyone with people I don't really know…and it's kind of intimidating." She turned to Jace and asked, "Are you sure it's alright with your family if I tag along on your vacation? I mean, it seems a bit forward for me to just barge in without an invitation." Gage would have laughed at her if he hadn't realized how serious she was. He'd forgotten she'd been raised in a world that was predicated on social standing and rules of etiquette he'd never understand.

Jace smiled warmly at her and captured her other hand in his, "Pet, we'll be lucky if we don't walk into a house full of people anxious to meet you. And my mom has no doubt been cooking for two days knowing *her boys* are coming home and bringing a special lady with them." Gage was grateful he'd asked her because she seemed to relax back into the seat.

By the time they rolled through the gates leading to the Garrett Ranch, Gage's stomach was already rumbling in anticipation and hunger. They had decided to forgo stopping in favor of Jace's mom's cooking. Before Logan had even put the vehicle in park, people were streaming out the front door. Gage heard Jace moan in frustration just as he, Logan, and Kalen all started laughing.

The five of them were enveloped with a flood of welcoming family and friends, including several of Gage's family members. But it was the shrill shriek from the door that caught everyone's attention. Gage watched as the crowd seemed to part as if Moses had just commanded it as Abby Garrett came down the stairs at a full run and launched herself into her big brother's waiting arms. "Indy, you're home…Finally!" All of Gage's friends loved Abby, she had quickly become a little sister to each of them. But as Gage watched the silent communication that seemed to be arching between Logan and Kalen, he had to wonder if that wasn't going to be changing—and sooner rather than later if he had to make a guess.

"Short Round. Damn, I'm glad to see you. But really little sister, we have to work on your shyness issues." Everyone around them burst into laughter, because God knew timid was not a word *anyone* would use to describe Abby Garrett. Gage shook his head at their nicknames for each other. After Jace had seen Abby collapse in the yard from an allergic reaction to penicillin, she'd dubbed him her hero and being the Indiana Jones fan that she was, the name Indy had stuck quickly. Jace had explained that he wasn't going to be outdone and the young Asian boy in the first movie had always reminded him of Abby, because the kid was wise beyond his years and too fearless for his own good, so she'd become Short Round.

Short fit Abby perfectly, but round she was not. Everyone that met Abby marveled at how tiny she was compared to her brute of a brother. At six and a half feet tall, Jace dwarfed most people, but beside him, his five foot sister looked like a Native American version of Tinkerbell. Once Jace finally set Abby on her feet she sprang into Gage's arms wrapping her arms around his neck to give him a huge hug. "I'm glad to see you, too, bonus brother." And then she whispered in his ear, "Is this you guys' girlfriend? Damn…way to go. Holly Mills is famous, ya know?"

For a few seconds, Gage was too stunned to speak. Were he and the rest of the security team so lost to the outside world that none of them had recognized her name? After Holly's accident, they'd done the security check that *should have been done* months earlier and been floored by what they'd learned. Hell, their little sub was an incredibly talented woman. Not only had she authored several commercially successful novels, she'd written too many screenplays to count, and was a well-known actress as well. But it had been her Mensa membership that impressed them all the most. While success was recognized by Gage and the other former Special Operations soldiers, intelligence was almost revered.

"As a matter of fact she is our girlfriend and I'll let you down so we can introduce you." Gage watched as Abby's eyes moved quickly to where Logan and Kalen were standing beside them. Both men were looking at Abby as if she was a gourmet meal and they were starving—*very interesting*. Jace made quick work of the introductions and then Pilar Garrett herded them all inside insisting they could continue visiting while they ate.

* * * *

Holly was sure she'd never seen so much food at a private party in her entire life. The backyard of the Garrett's home had obviously been designed for entertaining. The outdoor kitchen was set in an enormous circle of large boulders that had been smoothed on their tops so they doubled as seating. The flagstone floor was accented by dark gravel and the entire area was filled with blooming flowers and shrubs, some in brightly colored clay pots. The sun was just beginning to set and Holly watched in wonder as the entire backyard lit up with accent lighting.

She must have been standing with her mouth gapping open because Jace stepped up beside her and she heard his soft chuckle, "Do you like it? My mom loves to entertain and my dads love her, so when she asked for an outdoor kitchen they outdid themselves."

"It's amazing. I can't believe how beautiful it is and good grief there is so much food. How did one small woman manage to cook so much when I can't even toast bread without setting off the smoke detectors?" Holly realized the minute she'd spoken that was probably information she didn't need to share and she felt her cheeks flush with embarrassment.

Jace must have noticed her blush, because he pulled her into his arms and kissed her on the forehead before leaning close to her ear, "Pet, don't be worrying about cooking. You have plenty of incredible abilities and as your Doms, Gage and I plan to keep you too busy to cook anyway."

Holly felt her pussy flood with moisture and a flash of memory went through her mind so quickly she didn't have time to grasp it. Her sharp intake of breath must have alerted Jace because his expression darkened, "What's wrong, pet?"

"Nothing, I just had a blip of a memory race through my mind but it was so short and quick I didn't catch it." She sighed and then looked up, surprised to see his face lit in an enormous smile.

"Damn that's great news, baby. Let's go find Gage and share it with him as well. I know he's going to be very happy to hear it." Holly couldn't help but get caught up in Jace's enthusiasm, maybe this trip had been a good idea after all. She'd just realized that all of the problems she was facing hadn't entered her mind once since she'd arrived at the ranch.

Once they'd talked to Gage, they'd all three filled plates and settled down in a corner so they could watch the activities while they enjoyed their food. Holly noticed that both men seemed in much better spirits and she wondered if it was the fact they were being well-fed, surrounded by family and friends, or that she'd finally shown a small measure of progress.

She didn't even realize she'd spoken out loud until Gage leaned close and laughed, "It's all three, sweetheart. And by the way, that is also progress because you haven't spoken your thoughts out loud since the accident and that is something Master Jace and I both missed." Holly hadn't missed the *Master* comment and felt her pussy clench in response. Evidently her body's memory was better than her mind's.

Jace looked down at her and smiled, "Did your pussy just remind you that you belong to us, pet?"

Holly felt her face go hot and knew she was probably glowing in the dark. "H-how did you know that?"

"We are your Doms, pet, it's our job to know your body even better than you do." His smile seemed to have an underlying intent and the thought caused goose bumps to race up her arms as another spark of memory raced through just below the surface. "What were you just thinking, pet? Don't think about your answer, just say it."

"It was something familiar about you that just went by so quickly. It feels like something has flown by me, you saw it, but it was so fast, you can't describe it. Does that make sense?"

Gage leaned over and kissed the top of her bare shoulder. "It makes perfect sense, sweetness. And even better, it means your brain is healing and your memories are trying to surface. Don't force them, just let them bubble up on their own."

"Well, I sure wouldn't have ever thought I'd hear those words from you, Gage. Such poetic musings from the man whose personal philosophy was always 'Kill, then question'?" Holly couldn't contain her giggle as she watched Abby Garrett slide into a chair facing them. She'd liked Jace's sister the minute the young woman had taken a flying leap into her brother's outstretched arms. Holly had always dreamed of having a brother or sister, but her parents had been adamant that they weren't going to make *that mistake* twice.

"Short Round, you aren't too big to paddle, you know? And I think I might know just where to find a couple of volunteers for that job." Gage raised an eyebrow at Abby and Holly watched as the tiny beauty's face turned crimson, despite having inherited her mother's golden-tanned complexion.

Jace turned his full attention to his sister, "Abby? Who do I have to kill? What is Gage talking about?" Holly watched as he morphed into Alpha-Brother right before her eyes. *Oh damn, what a great line for a play. Or maybe a character in a book. I wonder what I can do with that.* Abby's snort of laughter brought Holly back to the moment but she wanted to dance for joy that her brain seemed to be kicking back into gear.

"Oh brother mine, don't you try going all Dom on me…I'm immune to your ways." The gleam in Abby's dark eyes was short-lived when Logan and Kalen pulled up chairs and sat on each side of her.

"Is that a fact? Well, that might be an interesting theory to test, Shorty. What do you think Logan? You think short-stuff here is immune to all things Dom? Wonder what her dads would say?" Holly was sure Kalen Black's voice must be what angels sound like, it had an almost mystical quality to it and it was easy to imagine him using it on the women Kat had told her the two men had shared. Holly watched Abby's eyes go wide and then dilate just before she started choking on the bite she'd just taken. Kalen patted Abby on the back several times before she finally seemed to right herself. "Damn Shorty, I didn't mean for you to get all choked up. You okay?"

"Yes and thanks for your concern…questionable as it may be. I assure you I am quite resilient to bossy men *because* I grew up with them." And then pointing at Holly, she added, "If you need any pointers on how to circumvent their system, let me know. I'll be happy to help."

"You're skating on mighty thin ice Short Round." Jace's voice was almost a growl and Holly's entire being stilled in response. He turned to her and smiled, "I wasn't snarling at you, pet." *Holy crap, how did he know?* He leaned over and kissed her sweetly, "It's my job to know."

Holly smiled and turned her attention back to her plate, deciding to stay out of the drama unfolding in front of her. But watching was really an interesting study in verbal versus non-verbal communication. It wasn't hard to imagine Kalen Black as a deadly enemy, his dark hair was a shade too long, giving him a classic bad-boy look. Holly had noted each time she'd seen him that his movements were so graceful they were almost catlike. It wasn't hard to see why the other men called him "pretty boy" because he was extremely good looking and there was a magnetism that seemed to surround him. If the electric current leaping between Kalen and Abby was any indication, Abby's steel was being pulled in fast and hard.

Abby had leveled her glare at her brother, "Listen, I've had about all of the Alpha male bullshit I can take, so back off big brother. I came home to escape this…" Holly watched as the woman's eyes filled with unshed tears that she quickly blinked away. "Frack…never mind. I need to go help mom." Smiling at Holly she added, "Come up tomorrow and we'll chat. I'm anxious to get to know you." With that she scrambled to gather up her things and before Holly could blink, Abby was gone.

Kalen looked at Jace, "What happened to her and what did she mean by escape?"

Chapter 17

Jace wasn't sure which was more startling—his sister's comments or the fact that his friends had both just essentially declared their interest in her. His confusion must have been apparent because he felt Holly's small hand on his forearm. "Jace, are you alright? You look kind of…well, stunned is the first word that comes to mind. Would you like for me to go check on Abby?" The kindness of her words and the sincerity in her expression warmed his heart and he fell just a little further in love with her.

"Yes, pet, I'd appreciate that very much. She seems to like you and I'm not sure I'm quite ready to talk with her." When she immediately started to stand up, he stilled her, "But don't be gone too long, baby. We need to be heading down to the guest house and getting you settled in. We promised to take care of you and that is exactly what we intend to do." She cupped his face in a move so tender you would have thought they'd been lovers for years. Holly didn't say anything, she simply nodded her head and then quickly made her way into the house.

Jace turned his attention to his friends and simply said, "Explain." There wasn't any heat in his demand, it was just a request for information. The bottom line was that Abby was a grown woman and short of someone deliberately hurting her, he wouldn't interfere in her life. Both men briefly spoke of their interest in Abby and assured her older brother that they had her best interest at heart, although it appeared she might not be on board yet.

Even though Abby was only twenty-five, she was a well-respected geo-engineer working in a male-dominated field. Her specialty was biofuels and she traveled so often he had trouble keeping tabs on her. After Jace had gotten Mitch Grayson to tap her smart phone with a tracking program that sent him updates about her location, Jace had finally been able to relax. At least now, if something happened, he'd know where to start looking for her.

Abby Garrett had always been academically advanced, and she'd driven their parents nearly insane with her constant thirst for information. They'd finally agreed to advanced placement for her in school and then had to hold on for the wild ride she'd given them. Jace had been deployed during the time Abby had blown through high school and college and graduate school—all in four years. She rarely copped to the fact that she had dual PhDs because, as she'd explained to him one night, it was just a pain in the ass to explain why she was so young and so smart. She'd snorted in disgust, "Cripes, how am I supposed to explain *that*? It just *is*." He'd laughed at the time because he'd understood her dilemma even though he also certainly understood everyone's confusion. Jace didn't even want to consider how bad something was if it was derailing the little pint-sized genius.

Jace looked between Kalen and Logan and groaned. He really didn't want to get involved in this, and quite frankly, it was the former Rangers that he was more worried about. He'd seen Abby in action and she could slice and dice a man before he even knew he was near a knife. Sighing, he just shook his head, "I don't really know what's going on. I know there was some kind of a problem at a drill site, but we just got here and I haven't had a chance to talk with either of my dads yet. Not that they'll know anything, but it's the only place I know to start. I know Abby just got here last night, so she wouldn't have wanted to distract mom with her problems. But I can't see her flying under the dads' radar, they don't miss anything, particularly when it comes to their daughter—something you might want to keep in mind."

Logan leaned back in his chair steepling his fingers in a move that should have look relaxed, but was anything but. "Why don't you and surfer-boy here take care of your sweet sub and let us spend a little time finding out what's up with Shorty?"

It was a testament to how worried he was about Holly that he readily agreed to Logan's suggestion. He simply nodded, "Agreed. But remember, she is my baby sister…"

Logan nodded once, "Got it, hurt her and die. Understood."

* * * *

Holly walked into the kitchen and froze. There were dirty dishes everywhere and the women in the kitchen were sitting around the table sipping wine as if they were oblivious to the fact they were surrounded by total destruction. She didn't even want to consider the hissy fit her own mother would be throwing about the state of her kitchen if it looked half this bad. Turning to the ladies she inquired about Abby and was directed down the hall to the den. She found Abby staring out a window overlooking the backyard, obviously lost in thought. Not wanting to startle her, Holly cleared her throat before walking up beside her.

"They send you to check on me? Shit, that sounded rude. I'm sorry."

Holly laughed, "Are you kidding? You are going to have to step up your game if you want to compete in the *Rude Olympics* with my mother. And no, I volunteered."

Abby burst out laughing and Holly watched as the woman's face went from tightly held sadness to bewitchingly beautiful in a heartbeat. "Damn I'm going to love having you around, sure hope those two don't fuck this up."

This time it was Holly's turn to laugh, "Truth is, it's more likely I'll be the one to mess up. I'm not working with a very good track record from what I understand." Looking at Abby she asked, "You okay? Anything I can do to help? I mean after all, I'm probably your best bet for a confidant since my memory seems to fade inappropriately leaving me staring off into oblivion like some spaced-out stoner." To Holly's great relief, Abby leaned her head back and roared with laughter. *God it feels good to be myself again...oh my God...this is one of the pieces that's been missing.*

Abby led Holly over to one of the smaller sofas and when they'd settled in, she explained some of the problems she'd been dealing with over the past few months at work. And even though Holly didn't understand all the technical issues Abby had rattled off like they were common knowledge, she did understand that two different men...from competing organizations...were making Abby's life hell. Even as little as Holly knew about the entire situation, she could clearly see the potential for danger, because there was simply too much money at stake.

"Don't you think you should talk to your family about this? Perhaps they'd have some ideas to help?" The minute she'd spoken the words she realized how inane they sounded. Rolling her eyes at her own foolishness she added, "Oh my God, listen to me. Of course they'll have suggestions...Alpha Doms are kind of a double whammy in the suggestion department I'm guessing."

"You got it in one. I know this could get ugly, I'm not the village idiot, but I really need to process it before I talk to anyone else about it. I appreciate your ear and I'll appreciate your amnesia even more." They shared a laugh and were just getting up to return to the party when Gage and Jace stepped through the door.

Gage walked up to stand right in front of Holly, while Jace stepped over and she heard him speaking quietly to his sister. Gage used his fingers under her chin to direct her attention to up to him. "Sweetness, you about ready to call it a night?"

Smiling up at him, she wondered how she'd gotten so lucky to have two gorgeous men taking such good care of her. Giving herself a mental head slap, she thought how literal that question was at this moment. She shook her head, "Not just yet, I need to help with the cleanup. Did you see that kitchen? Good Lord...I can't leave Jace's mom with that kind of a mess." Even though she'd been raised in a household filled with servants, Holly's Aunt Daphne had drilled etiquette into her from an early age and she'd always appreciated her aunt's efforts because watching her mother's behavior had always made Holly cringe.

Jace had walked up to her side and she heard him chuckle, "Pet, my mom has already marshalled the troops and the cleanup is nearly finished. If she had wanted you and Abby to help, believe me, there wouldn't have been a place on this ranch remote enough to hide the two of you. Now, let's go say our goodbyes and head out." He leaned down so that his quiet words were a warm breeze over her ear, "We've been waiting too long to feel your delectable naked body between us in bed, pet. We won't push the sex issue just yet, but naked in bed is non-negotiable."

Trying not to swoon on the spot and clenching her pussy tightly as if she could stem the burst of moisture that had just soaked her panties, Holly walked between Jace and Gage as they made their way back into the now sparkling clean kitchen. She stood by quietly while both men spoke with their families and friends hoping that her smile didn't look as plastic as it felt. Her entire body seemed to be vibrating from her core out and it was if her soul recognized them despite the fact her mind was busy playing catch-up. Holly was surprised to find out their bags had already been delivered to the guest house and that all they were left to do was make the short moonlit walk.

The guest house had a beautiful wraparound porch lined with potted plants. There was a porch swing that looked as if it would easily seat four or five people. When they stepped up to the door, Holly was a bundle of nervous energy. Jace handed the key to Gage and turned her into his arms, "Pet, look at me." She could feel him waiting for her to respond but it was taking all of her concentration to just keep from shattering like the finest crystal. It wasn't fear, but anticipation that seemed to be powering itself unchecked through her system. "Holly, do you remember the doctors telling you that you should expect exaggerated emotional responses while your body heals?"

His words penetrated the fog that had settled over her and she snapped her attention to his smiling face. "No. Really? I mean, no I don't remember hearing that. But it makes sense I guess and it makes me feel better, because I was feeling like…well, I don't want you to be disappointed in me." She hated the tears she felt running down her cheeks, but she couldn't help the wave of emotion that was threatening to pull her under.

When Gage opened the door and stepped to the side, she took one step toward him but he bent and scooped her up into his arms. Cradling her close he made his way down the hallway and into what she assumed was the master suite. The bed was enormous…much larger than a regular king-size. Even as tall as both he and Jace were, she was sure they'd be able to sleep comfortably in a bed this size. Gage didn't set her on her feet until he'd reached the bathroom. "We'll let you have a few minutes of privacy, but then we're going to join you in the shower. We need to get you into bed, sweetheart." His fingertips brushed the side of her face so softly she found herself leaning into his touch, seeking the comfort that it offered.

It didn't take her long to finish up and she was washing her hands when they walked back into the room. They made short work of setting out towels, starting the shower, and stripping themselves and then her. She gasped when she stepped into the shower…it was really more of a small garden room than a shower. The back wall was covered in what must be native stone because it looked like what she'd seen surrounding the outdoor kitchen. Tiny lights behind cascading water gave the waterfall a sparkling look that was almost hypnotizing. There were several tropical plants sitting on rock ledges and it seemed as if pulsing jets of water were coming from every direction. But it was the large overhead showerhead that simulated a gentle rain that was Holly's favorite feature. She had always loved walking in the rain. Standing there with her head tilted back so that the water could sluice over her face she felt like a child again, and even if it was only for a few seconds she was that carefree young girl once more…the one who hadn't yet learned she wasn't ever going to *be* enough or *do* enough to please her parents.

Chapter 18

Watching Holly tilt her face up to the water as it painted its way over her porcelain skin, Gage wondered what was going through her mind. Ordinarily, he or Jace would demand to know, but they knew she had been walking an emotional edge ever since Jace had told her she'd be sleeping naked between them. Gage had watched as their little sub's body had responded in all its submissive perfection all the while her mind had been racing. He'd been sure that her anxiety hadn't been from fear, because he'd seen the heat in her eyes. No, there hadn't been anything but arousal coursing through her veins, he was sure of that much.

Filling his palm with a generous amount of shampoo, Gage started working it through her long hair. He massaged her scalp and was rewarded by her soft moan of appreciation. "Do you like that, sweetness?" He chuckled when she groaned her agreement and pushed closer into his hands. By the time he'd shampooed and conditioned her hair, Jace had finished his shower and took over with Holly while Gage took his own shower.

Gage watched as Jace ran his soaped hands over every inch of Holly's skin in slow, sweeping strokes that he was sure were setting each and every nerve ending aflame. He and Jace had always known the value of touch when dealing with a submissive in their care. Gage had seen Doms fail miserably with a sub simply because they hadn't taken advantage of every opportunity to touch the woman they were supposed to be cherishing.

Leading Holly into the bedroom Gage was grateful to whoever had taken time to turn down the bed and adjust the lights so the room itself seemed to invite relaxation. There was soft piano music playing through the hidden speakers and Gage watched as Holly's eyelids began to droop before they'd even gotten her to the bed. She was so utterly wiped out that she seemed to have forgotten she was naked and they were both sporting hard-ons that could pound nails. Just as they'd settled her between them, she'd snuggled against his chest and pushed her ass against Jace's groin and murmured, "I've wanted you...both of you for so long. You promised...and I'm so sorry I ran. I just remembered him hitting me with his belt...and it hurt so badly."

Gage went completely still, barely daring to breathe because he didn't want to interrupt her. He pushed the hair from her face and kissed her forehead hoping it would be just enough to prompt her to continue. He was pleased when she took a shuddering breath. "The doctor called the police and I wanted to die when they took pictures of what he'd done to me. Mama was so mad at me for causing a fuss...and now I've done it again. I'm so sorry..." Her words had enraged him, but it was the utter defeat in her small voice that broke his heart.

Long after her breathing had evened out, Gage spoke quietly into the darkness, "I'll find him. There is no hole deep enough for him to hide in." Jace didn't answer, but he didn't need to, Gage already knew they were in agreement. And as heart wrenching as the information had been, it had also answered several important questions, as well as given them even more hope that Holly's memory was well on its way back. He wasn't entirely sure how he was going to find out who Holly had flashed back to when she'd seen him removing his belt, but it was obviously critical to find out exactly what had happened—the *who* was just going to be bonus information.

Gage felt Jace slipping from the bed, "I'm going to call Mitch Grayson. If anyone can access the records, it'll be him." Everybody knew that there wasn't a computer database on the planet that Mitch couldn't find his way into. The man was a techno-genius of the first order and the Lamont's chief of security and brother in law, Colt

Matthews was a very close second. The quiet snick of the door must have been enough to penetrate Holly's sleep because she immediately snuggled closer.

"Hmmm…Gage." He smiled to himself, happy that she obviously already recognized him, even in sleep. Pulling her closer to him, he pressed her soft curves against his body and lost himself in the wonder of her softness. There was a tremendous appeal to having a woman's warm naked flesh against your own and its significance wasn't lost on Gage.

* * * *

Jace wasn't surprised to find out that his own team was busy with activity at Club Isola, so his check-in with them had been short and sweet. His conversation with Mitch and Colt had taken longer. By the time Jace had finished recounting what Holly had shared, Mitch had already pulled up several reports related to an incident while Holly had been a student at a private boarding school in New England. Mitch and Colt had both been in the Crow's Nest at The ShadowDance Club when Jace had called. Colt's curses told Jace that he was helping Mitch and was equally disgusted with what they were finding.

Hearing how Holly had been beaten so severely by the Headmaster that her friends had snuck her out of the school during the night to get her to a local emergency room had turned Jace's stomach, but the photos attached to the responding officer's report had enraged him. She'd been sixteen at the time and her small body looked like that of a prisoner of war. Many of the lashes had broken the skin, but according to the report they hadn't been able to close them immediately because of severe swelling from the other welts.

Jace had seen her bare back and hadn't noticed any scarring, when he spoke that thought out loud, Mitch responded with a chuckle that didn't contain any humor at all. "Her mother was pissed that she had gotten herself into this mess and had caused herself to become 'disfigured.' Her word, not mine by the way. Anyway, a few months later, she sent Holly to Switzerland for plastic surgery."

"Why Switzerland? Christ, they have some of the world's leading plastic surgeons in New York."

"Seems the visit was twofold. Not only did her mother want the scars erased, but evidently Holly was exhibiting some post-traumatic stress symptoms and her mother wanted that addressed at a clinic that has a reputation for fiercely protecting the identity and medical records of its patients. Their records are *supposedly* hacker-proof. Fucking beginners, I was in and out of their system in less than a minute—and that included the time it took me to put everything I wanted in my backpack."

Jace shook his head at Mitch's dark humor as Colt's voice came over the speaker, "Yeah…yeah, you're fucking boy-wonder. Now give the man what he's after so he can get back to bed with his woman—hell, at least one of us oughta be getting some lovin' tonight." Jace had worked with Colt Matthews a few times on combined missions and knew when he started using slang it was straight-up sarcasm. He appreciated the man's efforts to break up the tension. It was obvious why his leadership skills were so well-respected.

"Damn, Matthews, what crawled up your ass? Oh yeah, now I remember, your woman and son are off enjoying some sun and fun, and you *chose* to stay home and work. Well, suck it up buddy, not my fault." This time Mitch's chuckle was sincere and Colt's answering growl made Jace smile for the first time since they'd begun their Skype call.

Jace watched as Colt seemed to zero in on the screen in front of him and frown. His muttered "fuck" put Jace on alert immediately. Colt Matthews's reputation for calm amidst chaos was nearly legendary, so anything eliciting that reaction wasn't going to be good news. "Seems there are several feeler threads out there tagged to

Holly. Your woman has a couple of well-established aliases related to work she's done—Christ the woman is busy. Anyway, several folks seem awfully anxious to get her back on-line because she makes them a lot of money. And they are actively looking for her." Jace watched as Colt typed quickly and immediately Jace's inbox started pinging. "I've forwarded you what I'm looking at, but I'll save you some time and give you the penny-tour. Her parents are leading the charge, seems they have some financial interests tied to Holly's ability to produce screenplays for the company her dad owns. The fact that he owns it isn't well-known and I'd wonder if she knows to be honest with you. Anyway, there are people on both coasts who would really like to find her, she has several works in progress and they don't seem to be happy about her disappearance."

Jace could hear Mitch muttering to the side and could hear him typing furiously on a nearby keyboard. "They were trying to track her cell phone, but I've diverted them for the time being. For a couple of days, they'll be looking for a guy in the mountains of Idaho. Yeah, let's see how *that* works out for ya' ass-hole." Jace knew Mitch was talking to his computer and smiled at his friend's ability to personify the devices he was working on. Mitch didn't miss a beat, "But in the meantime, you might want to get her a new phone and disable hers. I've already backed up everything from hers so don't worry about destroying it." Mitch finally looked up and smiled and Jace shook his head.

"Damn glad you're a friend and not my enemy Grayson."

"Keep that in mind, Garrett. I'm a real pain in the ass when I'm mad." Mitch's words didn't hold any heat, but Jace didn't doubt their accuracy for a minute.

Chapter 19

Laying in the warm sunshine alongside Abby Garrett listening to the soft swishing sounds of the family's pool was as close to blissful relaxation as Holly had enjoyed in far too long. Just knowing she didn't have to *do* anything today was enough to make her want to dance for joy. "Well, girlfriend, what's put that smirk on your face? And good Lord, please don't tell me anything intimate about my brother or bonus brother, because that would just be too much information, I assure you."

Holly laughed at Abby's comments, there wasn't any doubt, but what she and Abby were going to be great friends. The young woman's off-beat comments and observations alone were enough to endear her to Holly. "No, I was just thinking how good it feels to not be facing some looming deadline. I used to write because I loved it…and I had stories to tell, but now…Well, now the pressure to *produce* work has sucked a lot of the joy out of it. And since I've lost my cell phone somewhere, I haven't checked in to see what kind of nasty-grams await on voice mail, text and email." Holly didn't mention that she'd already closed her Facebook and Twitter accounts because the stalking had gotten so out of control.

When she looked over at Abby, she was surprised to see her new friend staring at her with a look of total disbelief on her face. "What the hell? Why are you allowing people to push you around like that? Oh brother, I'm really gonna have to teach you to step up your game, sister. You are entirely too nice, well, shit…of course you are…why else would you be hanging out with Tweedledum and Tweedledee."

Holly saw Jace and Gage standing behind Abby with their arms crossed over their bare chests and almost gasped, but Jace put his finger to his lips in a gesture for her to keep quiet. Looking back at Abby it was clear from the gleam in her eyes she knew full well they were standing behind her and intended to play with them a bit before letting them know it. "They're probably the most overly protective pair of testosterone beakers in the lab, if you know what I mean. Ah hell, better add Chip and Dale to that, too. Damn, they tried to interrogate me last night…as if." *Oh shit, I hope she knows what she's doing. And I really hope she knows Chip and Dale have joined her brothers.*

"Maybe they're worried about you? They all seemed concerned when you left the table last night."

Holly knew instantly that Abby was onto the game because she gave her a sly wink. "Oh sure, they're all worried because I'm meek and helpless. If you haven't been through Special Forces training you're a weak fool…oh woe is little ole me!" Holly nearly burst out laughing at Abby's dramatic southern imitation of Scarlet, complete with the back of her hand to her forehead. "Whatever would I do without them to look out for me? Why, I don't know a thing about birthin' no babies *or anything else* apparently."

Holly actually saw Gage's lips twitch as he suppressed a laugh and Jace's eyes rolled, but it was the growling from Logan and Kalen that had Abby breaking out into a fit of giggles. "You yo-yos wanna sneak up on a girl, then you need to choose one without a buddy sporting nice shiny sunglasses. Geez, no wonder this country is in big trouble if that is the most clandestine its operatives can be." Holly watched as Jace and Gage each took a step to opposite sides opening up a space for the other two men to step in. In a move so fast Holly barely caught it, they picked Abby up and tossed her unceremoniously into the pool and dove in after her.

Laughing out loud at the antics in the pool, Holly suddenly realized Jace and Gage were watching her rather than the craziness playing out in the water. She felt the heat of their combined gazes and her body responded as if it had been programmed to. Her nipples peaked so quickly she was sure they wouldn't miss the change because the thin fabric of the barely there suit Abby had leant her wasn't going to hide anything. Her pussy was suddenly soaking wet and she hoped they wouldn't notice the dampness that was probably already visible from the outside. The flush she felt working itself up her chest to her neck and then her face was going to be impossible to hide though.

"Take off the glasses, pet. We want to be able to see those beautiful eyes as need and lust race through you." Jace's voice was low and heavy…she was quickly recognizing it as his Dom-voice and her body responded before her mind even processed the words. So much for hoping they hadn't noticed her response to them. Lowering her glasses, she blinked at the bright sunshine.

"What's in your glass, sweetheart? Abby didn't fix you anything with alcohol in it, did she?" Gage's eyes hadn't left hers, but he'd obviously noted her margarita glass filled with limeade. Abby had deliberately chosen the bar glasses, saying it was just a way to *gig* her brothers.

"No…it's just limeade." She wouldn't have had an alcoholic drink anyway, but she wasn't going to share all of that with them just yet. Holly had found out a long time ago, that once a man found out alcohol worked as truth serum on her, he was usually all too eager to use that information to his advantage. And with these two, Holly knew she was going to have to retain any advantage she could, because they obviously had a lot of experience with things she had only dreamt about.

Jace held out his hand to her, "Come on, pet, let's get in the pool. I want to enjoy the water before Abby stops playing with those two and shows them what all those years of self-defense training have taught her."

Gage laughed, "Yep, probably going to be blood spilled before long, so let's enjoy it while we can."

Holly placed her hand in Jace's much larger one and felt Gage's hand fit against the small of her back. The feel of his palm against her bare skin sent a shiver through her, and the wave of lust that followed it nearly brought her to her knees. *Oh brother, how do they do that? Why does my body seem to know them?*

Jace pulled her flush against his chest and leaned down so that he was speaking against her ear, "Your body recognizes its Masters, pet. You are a submissive—it radiates from your very core. Have you noticed that you don't respond like that to Kalen or Logan?" Her mind was racing and she suddenly realized he was right. Her sudden intake of breath must have been answer enough, because his chuckle was rich, "They are Doms, too, pet. But your body is already programmed to Gage and my commands alone. Some of the club's subs respond to any Dom, but that isn't who you are, is it, my love?"

Her voice sounded airy and light even to her own ears, "No...no, it's not. It's just you and Gage. I don't understand it...not really, but I recognize it." She felt Gage step up behind her, pulling her back against his chest he wrapped his arms around her.

"Are you wet for us, sweetness?" When he slid his fingers under the top of her bikini bottom and through her slick folds, there was no hiding the truth. "Oh, baby, you are soaking wet." She couldn't stifle the soft groan that came from deep in her chest as his finger circled her clit. "I think our sweet sub needs some relief, Master Jace. What do you think? Should we help her out?" Holly suddenly remembered that they were standing out in the open...right in Jace's parents' backyard for God's sake. *His parents will think I'm some two dollar hooker they picked up from some seedy bar.*

* * * *

Gage had felt the instant Holly realized they were out in the open because every muscle in her lush little body had gone on alert, but her whispered words had shocked him. Was she fucking serious? For just a few seconds he wasn't sure Jace had heard her, but when he looked up at his friend he saw the fire in his eyes. "Pet, you may not remember it, but you were warned about these self-deprecating comments. We want them to stop—right now. And remember, pet, my mom has been married to two men for almost forty years. I'm absolutely sure knowing that Gage is finger-fucking you and I'm watching is not going to shock her."

"Well, it seems our little sub enjoys this type of play. Feeling your sweet honey coat my fingers while you listen to your Master is a huge turn-on, baby. Right now my cock is aching to slide through these folds, just like my fingers are—close your eyes and listen to my words, sweetness." Gage felt Holly stiffen again and then her knees buckled. He was grateful he'd already had her tucked against him because she didn't drop more than an inch before he had her.

Jace stepped up and cupped her chin, "Pet? Are you alright?"

She seemed to sag in Gage's arms as she relaxed. "Oh yes, it's just that…well, I remember this. I mean, we've done this before, and I remembered it. Master Gage's words…his hold…his touch, well it brought it all crashing back so suddenly I couldn't believe it." Now it was Gage's turn to sag, but his was pure relief.

Jace was stroking his fingers along the side of Holly's face and smiling down at her. Gage was sure his friend was giving him a minute to regroup. Jace knew the guilt he'd been plagued with over Holly's injury and Gage was certain his friend wouldn't have missed the wave of emotion that he was sure had been in his expression. "Well, this is cause for celebration. We'll talk about exactly how much has come back to you in a few minutes, my sweet pet. But first, I'd like very much to watch your lovely face as Master Gage makes you come."

Gage wanted nothing more than to feel her shatter in his arms—well, maybe it would be better if he was buried inside her sweet ass, but this was going to work just fine. Moving his fingers through her smooth pussy he pressed his lips against her neck just below her ear and felt her pulse kick up. "Spread your legs just a bit, sweetness. Good girl, we want Master Jace to be able to hear the sweet slurps your wet cunt makes as my fingers fuck you. Your greedy pussy is milking my fingers, tugging them in and then tightening around them like a fist trying to keep them inside you. You have no idea what that does to your Dom, baby. Knowing that I am fine tuning your body to respond to my touch gives me great pleasure."

Knowing he'd already gotten her to the point that she was hovering just before cresting over the edge of orgasm was pure joy. Gage listened to Jace telling her that she wasn't allowed to come without their permission, he smiled when she gasped. "Hold it, pet, it'll be all the sweeter. And when you come, we want to hear your screams, don't you dare deny us the pleasure of hearing your orgasm. Do you understand?"

When she didn't immediately respond to Jace's question, Gage watched as he lowered his fingers to her tightly peaked nipples. Holly moaned at Jace's touch but still hadn't answered. When she jerked in his arms and her pussy flooded his hand, Gage knew Jace had pinched the nipples he'd been rolling between his fingers. "Pet? I asked you a question. You need to always answer the questions we ask you. Answer immediately and with complete honesty. Oh—and love, remember what we told you earlier, lying by omission will always be considered lying."

"Yes, I understand. I'll be embarrassed screaming in front of your sister and friends, but if that's what you want..." Gage knew she hadn't noticed the other three had stepped around the side of the hedge to the small bar area, so they weren't in view of anyone else at the moment. But her agreement to do as he'd commanded, despite her misgivings, was a gift he intended to reward.

"Such a good girl. Now, let's see what we can do about that release your body needs so badly." Jace smiled up at him, and Gage knew his grin was reflecting how pleased he was that his cock would soon be sliding in through the thick honey now flowing over his fingers. Her soft gasp as his callused fingers worked their magic on her gave Jace his next cue. "Now, while we have your undivided attention, I'll be asking you a few questions." Gage felt her entire body tense as she tried to focus her attention on Jace rather than the pleasure her body was chasing. He knew she was worrying she wouldn't be able to track the conversation much longer. And she was right, but he knew Jace didn't intend for his conversation to last long either.

"Are you on birth control, pet?"

"Um…yes, to regulate my cycle."

Gage was pleased that she'd answered so completely and knew Jace was too. "Your complete answer pleases me, pet. You're obviously a very bright woman and I can see how fast you're learning. Now, when is the last time you had sex?" Obviously, Jace was trying to find out just how much of that night had come back to her, because they both already knew the last time she'd had a cock. "We already know you're clean, because your recent hospital stay provided an abundance of information. Don't look so shocked, you were registered as Holly Garrett or didn't you notice that fact?"

"Oh my, no…I didn't know that. But…why?" Gage could feel her confusion and wanted to put it to rest quickly so they could get on to the main event.

"It was Daphne's idea. It was a way to shelter you from the media I suspect. Now, about that sex question—when was the last time, pet?" The answer didn't actually matter, but he'd like to see her have at least one orgasm under her belt before he slid into her so her muscles would be relaxed and well lubricated. While Jace was a bit longer, Gage's cock was wider and was definitely going to stretch her tender tissues.

"Years...three...well, almost four. But it's all good, because I'm pretty sure I remember the ba...basics. Oh my God."

Gage smiled at her because she was obviously regaining some of her sense of humor, something her Aunt had told them she had noticed was missing since Holly's accident. And it was obvious his fingers were hitting all the right spots. Gage knew she had just given Jace the perfect opening, "Well, as a matter of fact, pet, it hasn't actually been that long. I have already had the pleasure of feeling your pussy milking every ounce of seed from my body, so it is going to be Master Gage who slides into your hot pussy. But first, let's get you ready, shall we?"

Not missing the cue, Gage began fucking her with his fingers. He added another finger and then slid in a third so that he was using three of his long thick digits and he could feel her go liquid around them and knew she was on the cusp of release. Leaning down he bit down on the spot where her soft shoulder met her neck just as he heard Jace's growled, "Come for us, pet."

Chapter 20

Holly's response was instantaneous and explosive. Gage felt her honey rush over his fingers and was thrilled with her response. But it was her words that had rocked his soul, her stuttered, "Oh my God, Gage, *yes, please*" had bound his heart to hers in that instant. To hear his name cross her lips at the moment she let down every defense and found her release was pure perfection. While Jace squatted down and removed the bikini bottoms, Gage slid his own suit down and kicked it free.

Placing the flat of his palm between her shoulder blades, Gage stepped up pressing his throbbing erection firmly into the crack of her ass, letting her feel what she'd done to him as he bent her at the waist. At the same time, he saw Jace removing his own trunks and stroking his fist up and down his own length. "Spread those lovely legs apart, baby. Let me in. I'm going to fuck you while you suck Master Jace."

"Pet, have you taken a man into your mouth before?" Gage was sliding the bulging head of his cock through her soaking labia and battling the urge to slam it home. He saw Holly shake her head and he watched Jace smile down at her indulgently. "Well, I'm honored to be your first, love. Stick out that pretty pink tongue and lick the head. Oh yea, pet, that feels wonderful. Let me guide you, but don't get so wrapped up in following instructions that you forget to enjoy the sensations you'll be experiencing as well. Because I promise you, Master Gage fully intends to take you right back up that mountain and give you everything your body is clamoring for even as we speak."

Gage resumed slowly sliding the head of his cock through her folds, holding tight at the base trying to delay his own launch over the edge into ecstasy. He saw her tongue dart out yet again and then watched as Jace's eyes nearly rolled back in his head. Gage wanted to smile, but knew he was going to be on that same boat the minute he slid into her hot little cunt. Leaning over her, he nudged the head just inside as he rolled her nipples firmly between his fingers and then tugged. Her groan caused Jace to lean his head back and Gage heard him moan, "*Oh fuck*" just as his own cock pushed in to the hilt and he groaned the same words.

Feeling the heat of her pussy as it squeezed his bare cock was sweet torture. He hadn't fucked a woman without a condom since his first sexual experience as a young teenager and he'd longed for the sensation ever since. "Our woman feels like heaven. Her pussy walls are flexing around my cock and it feels like a beautiful silken vise. Jesus Christ on a crutch. I'm not going to last long at this rate and I want her to go first." Gage knew his voice sounded like he'd been eating glass, but it had taken every bit of control he'd had just to keep from pounding into her until he lost himself in her sweet body.

"Time to fly, pet, and I want you to take me with you. Will you swallow my seed?" Gage had just registered the words when he felt her pussy clamp down on him to the point it was nearly painful and her softly moaned assent had elicited a growl from Jace.

Gage reached around her and began circling her clit with his fingers while moving in and out of her with strokes that were quickly becoming faster and less controlled. Pinching her clit between his fingers slick with her cream, he spoke against her ear, "Now, sweetheart. Come for us." Her scream was muffled by Jace's cock sliding in and out of her mouth and she'd just taken a quick breath when he heard Jace groan his own release. Feeling her muscles still fluttering frantically around him, Gage shifted the angle a bit and sent her over the edge again and this time he followed her into bliss. Watching as fireworks exploded behind his eyelids, Gage wasn't sure how long his knees were going to hold him upright as the most explosive orgasm he'd ever had just kept crashing over him in wave after sweet wave.

When he was finally able to focus again, Gage realized that he was still buried inside her, but Jace had withdrawn and was kneeling in front of her whispering sweet words of praise against Holly's lips. Gage finally managed to withdraw and wanted to beat his chest as he watched their combined releases leaking from her swollen pussy. Grabbing a small towel he'd set off to the side, he quickly cleaned her and then himself before pulling his swim trunks back on. Gage watched as Jace stood up and pulled her into his arms hugging her tightly before he turned her back to him. Seeing the well-fucked and sated expression on her face was enough to please any man. Her eyes were half-lidded and she looked like she could curl against him and fall asleep standing up. As much as Gage would have loved to carry her all the way to the guest house naked, they would have to walk by a couple of barns and a mechanics shop that had ranch employees working in them, so he quickly wrapped her in a soft towel.

Scooping her up into his arms he kissed her on the forehead, "Baby, you are a dream come true. That was un-fucking-believable. You can swim later—maybe in a week or two—right now we're not finished exploring the delicious secrets of your body."

* * * *

From the moment the men had walked up to her as she soaked up the sun alongside Abby, Holly's body had been almost vibrating with need. And every single word they'd spoken and each touch had set her insides on fire. She had listened as Rissa and Kat raved about the joys of ménages, but *holy shit*. The first orgasm had been amazing, she had literally seen stars. But when Gage slid into her she knew it wasn't going to hold a candle to what was to come and she had been right.

The feel of Jace's cock pushing through her lips, the taste of him, and the sweet smell of musky man had been so much she'd almost come from that alone. Using her tongue, she had tried to feel each bump, ridge, and vein. The smooth head had pushed clear to the back of her throat, but she'd remembered what the girls had said about breathing through her nose and opening her throat. Oh…and the first time she had swallowed around him, she had known exactly what Kat had meant by him seeming to grow bigger right in that moment.

When he'd come down her throat she'd tasted his salty essence as his flavor had burst over her taste buds. The feeling of power, of knowing *she* had given him that pleasure had been heady indeed. Then Gage had pinched her clit and sent her straight over the moon. If he hadn't had ahold of her hips, she wasn't sure she would have stayed upright. And then when she'd felt his seed jetting against her cervix it had been enough to put her back on top of the wave again.

He'd left her bent over so long she had begun to worry, but when she noticed his ragged breathing, she was sure he'd been as affected as she had by the earth shattering climaxes they'd given her. When he'd pulled out and she'd felt their cum running down the inside of her legs she'd been embarrassed until she'd heard him growl "fucking beautiful." When he'd cleaned her she'd hidden her face in Jace's chest in sheer mortification. But he had explained that it was their right and privilege to take care of her. And even though it had still seemed weird, his words had made it seem a little more understandable and "normal." *Now there's a concept that's never going to be the same…the new normal is a whole lot different than anything I've ever even dreamed possible.*

She'd told them that her memory had come crashing back…all of it in one swift wash. And now that it was restored, she remembered that she still owed Gage four swats. And she intended to get that behind her…literally…as soon as possible. That was something both her friends had emphasized…the importance of getting punishments out of the way so they weren't hanging over your head impeding your pleasure.

Suddenly realizing that both Katarina Lamont and Rissa Grayson-Davis had managed to convince her that they were college pals made her chuckle to herself. She couldn't wait to thank them for their gift of friendship. It had been that connection that had gotten her through the first couple of days when the only people she'd known were Aunt Daffy and Ian. Callie and Ian had delayed leaving on their honeymoon until they'd known she was going to be alright...they would both always hold a special place in her heart.

Thinking about all that had happened was almost overwhelming. No doubt there were going to be some hard questions to answer about her meltdown and that wasn't a conversation she was looking forward to, but she wouldn't lie to Jace or Gage about it either. It had been all the various levels of truth in her life that had gotten her into such a fragile state that she'd barely held it together, and she had no desire to return to any of that...ever.

The feeling of being cradled in Gage's arms was almost enough to make her postpone the things she needed to say to them, but in the end she knew her desire for transparency was going to win out. She had only begun exploring this lifestyle, but there was something in it that spoke to her on a level so deeply ingrained in her heart she wasn't even sure how to describe it. The feeling of freedom that she'd known in that moment of complete surrender had been the most exhilarating moment of her entire life.

She suddenly realized she was standing naked in the bedroom of the guest house and both men were standing with their arms crossed over their massive chests watching her intently. *Oh crap on a cracker...I wonder how much of that I said out loud. Damn, I really need to get a handle on that habit.*

Chapter 21

It took everything Jace had to suppress his smile at Holly's self-admonishment. He was thrilled with the fact that she spoke her thoughts aloud and he knew Gage was as well. "In answer to your question, pet, I'd venture that you actually spoke most of that aloud. But I'd have to say that both of your Masters would just as soon it was a habit you didn't make any effort to break for a couple of reasons. First, it gives us a chance to get to know the real you in unguarded moments and second, it pleases us to hear just exactly how in touch with your feelings you are. Now, let's do first things first. Since it is obvious you remember the swats you owe Master Gage, we're going to get those out of the way and get them off your mind." The flash of fear he saw in her eyes told him he'd made the right decision, she wasn't going to relax until this was taken care of.

Gage held out his hand and she timidly placed hers in it and let him lead her over to a chair in the sitting area. Jace watched as Gage sat and pulled Holly around so that she stood along his right side. Moving closer, Jace leaned against the stone fireplace and watched as the scene played out in front of him. From where he stood, Jace would be able to monitor her face during her punishment. After the cluster fuck the other night they weren't going to take any chances with their precious little sub.

Jace watched as Gage held her hand in his for long seconds as he studied everything about her. A loving Dom watched every detail, and always noted any differences from one moment to the next. It was critical that the Dominant partner assure that the changes were going to get the sub in their care exactly where they needed to go during the scene. Even from where he stood, Jace noted the pulse at the base of her neck was faster than it had been a few minutes ago and her respiration rate had kicked up as well. Gage spoke to her softly, but there was no mistaking the Dom-tone of his words, "Sweetness, tell me why you are being punished."

Holly's eyes filled with unshed tears, "Because I called you a bastard in Italian. And…well, I just want to say, that after meeting your family…I'm really sorry. They are so nice and you were right when you said your mom wouldn't like it. Well, I guess I don't know so much about 'like it,' but she sure doesn't deserve any kind of judgment from me." Jace bit the inside of his mouth to keep from smiling, because Gage's mom was a tough cookie and had no doubt said the same thing to him in English more than once.

"While I agree with you, that my mom doesn't deserve anyone's judgment—the real reason I'm punishing you is because it was extremely disrespectful. And most of that is based on the fact that you didn't think I would understand what you'd said. You're only getting four swats because this is all so new to you, but I promise you this, sweetheart—you pull a stunt like that again and the punishment is going to be exponentially more severe. Are we clear?" Gage had been tracing circles on the inside of Holly's wrist the entire time he'd been speaking to her. Jace knew Gage was monitoring her heart rate even though he'd never taken his eyes from hers.

"I understand. And I am so sorry I disappointed you." Jace watched the tears stream down her face and knew Gage's swats wouldn't be what they would ordinarily have been because it was obvious she was already punishing herself way more than they ever could. Jace had only known a handful of subs who didn't really require much in the form of physical punishment, because their desire to please their Dom was so deep that any perceived disappointment was much more powerful as a deterrent. Now that wasn't to say those same subs didn't get off on erotic spanking or that you couldn't send them straight into sub-space with a good flogging followed by a few lashes of a single-tail whip. But since the difference between erotic pain and punishment pain was largely in the mindset of the submissive, it was all a huge continuum.

The essence of all Dominant/submissive relationships was actually fairly simple. Every bit of power a Dom had over a submissive was a gift the sub freely chose to give his or her Dom. He and Gage had talked endlessly about their commitment to the tenets of safe, sane, and consensual in every D/s encounter. It was the base-line of all BDSM play and absolute law at Club Isola.

The fact that they hoped to build a lifetime relationship with Holly and she was still so new to the lifestyle meant that they would be monitoring everything even more carefully than usual. Luckily they'd both been close to the "inside" of Ian's relationship with Callie and had gotten a rare glimpse at what it looked like to *get it right.*

Jace watched Gage position Holly over his lap and chuckled at her small shriek when she'd been shifted forward so that her toes were off the floor and her ass was peaked in the perfect position for Gage's hand. "Sweetness, this is not an erotic spanking. This is a punishment and as such, the swats are harder and I'll remind you that you are not allowed to come without permission." Jace could practically hear her mind screaming that he was insane. She'd learn soon enough that, done right, even a punishment spanking could send a sub over the edge of orgasm.

Gage had never been one to draw out a punishment, preferring to get it done and move on, so Jace wasn't surprised to see him land four well-spaced slaps in quick succession. Holly had probably barely had time to process the pain of the first swat by the time the last one had fallen. Gage's large handprints were clearly visible and they'd need to watch her carefully for bruising. Holly had been in the hospital after her last spanking and they had both been grateful her physician had been a Dom, so he hadn't documented the vivid handprints that had covered her sweet ass. Both Jace and Ian had learned quickly that

Callie bruised quite easily. Hell, the first spanking she'd gotten had turned her black and blue for several days.

Jace watched as Holly hiccupped her sobs after Gage settled her bright red ass on his lap. She'd hissed when her still burning skin had made contact with Gage's shorts, but had snuggled against Gage's chest and seemed to be settling down, so Jace moved into the bathroom to start the shower. Her sobs were more about her inner struggle than any pain she might have experienced. And as any good Dom would tell you, letting a sub release that pent up emotion was every bit as important as correcting bratty behavior.

By the time he had everything ready, Gage was walking through the door with her in his arms. For the first time, Jace noticed Gage was truly disheartened by a punishment he'd had to mete out. But his friend would have known the importance of keeping his word, he'd told her she was getting the spanking and if Gage was to have her trust, she needed to know he would do exactly what he'd said he would do—even if he no longer wanted to.

Jace stepped up to Holly and pulled her against his chest. Holding her softness, he realized how much he had craved moments exactly like these. After years of spending time in every shit-hole around the globe Uncle Sam could send him into, the simple joy of holding a curvy, naked woman wasn't lost on him. Pulling back, he cradled her blotchy, red face between his palms and smiled because she was still stunningly gorgeous despite all evidence of her crying jag. "Feel better, pet?"

"Y-yes, sir."

Holly's soft words sent his blood racing south and as he pushed out of his swim trunks, he knew there would be no hiding that fact— not that he really cared much to try. "See what you do to me, pet? But don't just look at my cock, love, look deep in my eyes and you will see the same thing in them that you see in Master Jace's." Her eyes went wide and then flooded with a longing that was unmistakable.

"You are beautiful, inside and out, pet. Your submissive nature and your responsiveness is a siren's call to both of us."

"Sweetness, you are exactly what Master Jace and I have spent years looking for. We'd always dreamed of finding you, but had begun to think you were just a wishful figment of our imaginations. We want to teach you about our lifestyle, but more importantly we want to teach you that you're stronger than you believe yourself to be. And if you'll let us, we'll protect and cherish you. The only thing we ask for in return is your submission and your loyalty. We'd like to feed you a line of bullshit that we'll only demand your submission during scenes, but it simply wouldn't be the truth." Gage was absolutely right and Jace was glad he'd put it out there.

"What do you mean? Like, you'll tell me where I can go and who I can see? Or what I can write? Oh, I could never agree to that." Jace watched her pull her bottom lip between her teeth and chew on it as she slipped out of the moment and started pacing the length of the room. *It could have been so wonderful, but I can't give up everything just to have spectacular sex. Although the idea of somebody helping me keep the wolves at bay is pretty appealing. Well, fuck a fat fairy. It was all so close too.* Her heavy sigh tugged at Jace's heart.

He looked up at Gage and saw nothing but indulgence. Gone was the Dom who would have delivered a blistering spanking because his sub was *gone* for a few moments. And in his place stood a Dom who had found his mate. Jace knew that Gage was a clear reflection of his own image. Obviously they weren't doing a very good job of training her if she thought they were planning to control her every move—and it was past time to clear up a few things.

Chapter 22

Boy if that didn't just about frost her cookies Holly didn't know what would. Here she'd been so close to having wild monkey sex again only to find out she was going to have to give up everything and become their little zombie sex-slave if she wanted to go any further. Damn it all to hell in a Honda anyway. She wasn't going to wear some skank-wear or eat from a bowl on the floor or any of the other crap she'd seen on the websites she'd browsed through. She had enough people in her life willing and all too able to dish out humiliation, she sure didn't need to sign up for more.

When she finally stopped pacing she looked up at them and just whispered, "I'm sorry. If you can help me call a cab…or maybe Abby could drive me to the airport…but I really think it's time for me to suck it up and get back to my real life." Damn, she had barely been keeping her head above water before, and now that she'd lost so many days, she was probably on everyone's shit list. Well, she'd dodged her responsibilities long enough.

Turning toward the closet, Holly had only taken a couple of steps when Jace's voice boomed through the room, "Stop right there, pet." She wanted to slap her palm against her forehead when she realized she had obeyed without even thinking. Damn, she was already behaving like a dog they'd taken to obedience classes, she shuddered to think what else she might do if…*Oh my God…they called it training, but I never even considered that it would be like this.* She felt herself sway at the realization that they had actually already started training her and she hadn't even realized it.

* * * *

While Jace was all for gathering all the information they could by allowing her to rant unchecked, he was beyond frustrated with her continuing misconception. And the worst part was that he and Gage had no one but themselves to blame. They'd shared subs at the club before and had never failed to find out their soft and hard limits and negotiate the scene in advance. So why the hell were they fucking up with the only sub who had ever *really mattered*? Mentally shaking his head at the absurdity of it he looked over to see the same look of frustration on Gage's face. Nodding his face toward the sofa, he knew Gage understood and they both grabbed one of Holly's elbows and led her in that direction.

Settling her on the coffee table so that she was facing them with her legs spread wide so they could view her glistening folds, they directed her to grasp her wrists behind her back so that her beautiful breasts were lifted in offering to them. "Why do I have to sit like this? I look like a slut for heaven's sake. You can't possibly be serious about having a conversation like this." *Ah, I do believe thou dost protest too much, sweet lady.*

Jace smiled at her and nodded, "We do indeed expect exactly that. And I'll caution you to watch your tone, sweet sub. We'll be keeping a careful count of the punishments you rack up. Now, the first thing we need to clear up is your misconception about what our expectations are for you."

"Sweetness, we want to add to your life, not take away from it. Now, you need to know we'll be quick to step up to the plate if we feel you are overextending yourself to the point it is causing you either physical or emotional distress, and we won't be subtle about it. Our job as your Dominants is to cherish and care for you, and to see to it that you always get exactly what you need."

Jace was sure Gage had intentionally left him the perfect opening. "Keep in mind, pet, that what you want and what you need may not always be the same thing. But since you have placed yourself in our care, it will be our responsibility and honor to care for you—in *all* ways."

Gage's expression seemed to soften and Jace watched as his friend leaned forward and gently pushed Holly's knees back apart. She probably hadn't even been aware that she had been slowly drawing them back together. But the message her body was sending was crystal clear, she was uncomfortable and drawing in on herself. Jace would be willing to bet, she had been basically left to her own devices long before she'd been out of grade school. It was a miracle she hadn't fallen in with the wrong group of rich kids and gotten mixed up in drugs or worse.

"Don't hide yourself from us, baby. We know this is new for you, but if I have to correct that behavior again, we'll have to figure out a way to secure those pretty legs in the position we've put them." Both men watched as a fresh stream of Holly's sweet cream moistened her pussy lips. She must have noticed them watching because her face was absolutely the brightest shade of crimson he'd ever seen when he looked up at her.

"We want to talk to you about hard and soft limits, pet. Do you know what those are?"

"Yes, sir. I think so. Hard limits are things I absolutely do not want to do or even try, like body fluids, knives, blood, cages, and humiliation. And soft limits are things that scare me, but that I might be willing to try at some point, like wax play." By the time she had finished her answer he noticed her breathing was once again becoming rapid and her pulse had spiked.

"Very good, pet. Master Gage and I appreciate your candid answer. And for now, that is enough information for us to start. Here is what we'd like to propose to you. We'd like for you to commit to a three-month long training. At the end of that time, we'll all sit down and re-evaluate and decide how we'll proceed." Jace was surprised to see tears fill her pretty green eyes, "Pet, tell me exactly what you heard, right now. Because we obviously have a serious communication problem." Jace kept his voice steady despite the fact he was desperate to find out what on earth she was thinking.

"I'm sorry, I know you only agreed to show me the ropes…and I shouldn't have expected anything more…and I didn't think I had let myself slip over that edge, but obviously I had. And well hearing you put a time limit on our time together was just so blatant." Jace watched her take a deep bracing breath before she went on, "I'm tired of living my life from the sidelines though, so if three months is all there is for us, then I'll take it. I won't lie to you, it will be hard to let go, but I promise I won't make it ugly."

By the time Holly had finished speaking Jace wasn't sure who he was angrier with—and there were several prime candidates. First of all, he was furious at her parents for their irresponsible parenting. How could parents with such an amazing daughter continually make her feel as if she wasn't *enough*? And he was frustrated with her for not recognizing how deeply both he and Gage had fallen for her. But most of all, he was disappointed in himself. How could he have let her believe she was only a temporary stop in his and Gage's lives?

* * * *

Gage rarely stepped in when Jace was leading with Holly because he respected his friend's experience with permanent ménage relationships, and quite frankly, this was just too important to risk. But it was obvious that Jace was holding on by a thread. The muscles in Jace's jaw were clenched so tightly that Gage was worried the poor bastard was going to shatter his teeth. Gage was sure most of Jace's anger was self-directed, but he doubted that would be how Holly would see it. All their sweet woman would see would be the explosion and with her deep desire to please those she cared about, Holly would no doubt place the entire burden of her Master's anger directly on her own shoulders.

Scooting to the edge of the sofa, Gage pulled Holly closer and held out his hand. "Give me your wrists, Holly." He'd used her name deliberately and watching her eyes widen in response, he knew she hadn't missed the change. He watched her wince as she moved her arms back in front of her so that she could lay her wrists in his upturned palm. Gage silently cursed himself for leaving her in that position for so long without checking on her, and he was relieved to find her fingers were still warm and pink so at least her circulation hadn't been compromised.

Her eyes were the most amazing shade of green and their shade was ever-changing, depending on her mood and level of arousal. Right now they were so filled with sadness his heart clenched knowing that he and Jace were responsible. "Sweetness, I'm afraid your Masters have done a very poor job of meeting one of the most basic principles of our lifestyle. We have clearly not adequately communicated exactly what we meant by the three month limitation."

Taking a deep breath, Gage decided to just go for broke and tell the fragile soul sitting before him exactly what he and Jace had planned. "You see, both Master Jace and I want this to be a permanent relationship. We'd like to marry you. Well, you would actually marry Jace in a civil ceremony, because he is older. But the ceremony we would all consider binding would be the commitment ceremony that would follow. In our hearts we would both be your husbands, sharing equally in the responsibilities and joys that bond brings."

Watching as the sadness that had painted her expression slowly changed to hope, Gage slowly released the breath he hadn't even known he was holding. "We wanted to give you the three months as a 'trial period' but it was intended as a chance for you to decide if you wanted us, not the other way around. Sweetness we already know that we want you in our lives forever, but you have been through a lot and we didn't want to overwhelm you." This time when the tears came, Gage was sure that they were tears of joy, but he wasn't leaving anything to chance. Reaching up to thumb away her tears, he was relieved to see her shy smile. "I sure hope those are happy tears, sweetheart."

* * * *

Holly didn't hesitate to show Gage that her tears were indeed, tears of pure joy. She heard his soft chuckle when she scrambled onto his lap and buried her face in his chest and clung to him like a vine. "Yes, they are tears of joy. I was so afraid you didn't want me and it was going to break my heart to have to walk away from you both. I really had no idea how I would be able to do it, but I wanted to treasure each moment…so if three months was all I could have, well, then it was just going to have to be enough."

The feel of his large, callused palm rubbing soothing circles over her bare back was a balm to her soul. She wasn't sure she fully understood why surrendering to them made her feel fulfilled but it reminded her of the joy she'd always found in placing the last piece of a jigsaw puzzle in place. Holly knew there were never any guarantees in any relationship because people's lives are never static…they grow and change. But she knew what the three of them shared was worth the risk.

Chapter 23

Standing up for Holly as she'd married Jace had been one of Abby's happiest moments. She and her brother had always been incredibly close, so seeing him this happy brought her joy as well. Who could have guessed that their relationship would progress so quickly? It had only been a week since Kalen and Logan had whisked her away from the pool area so Jace and Gage could seduce Holly. That had been a very interesting afternoon, indeed.

Leaning back against a rock wall in her parents' backyard watching as couples danced following the commitment ceremony that had given Holly a second husband, Abby watched from the shadows as Gage danced with his new bride. Holly was an amazing woman, and she and Abby had hit it off immediately. How her brother and bonus brother had managed to score such a talented and famous wife was a mystery to Abby. Smiling at her own mental joke she let her mind drift back to the afternoon she had almost given in to her attraction to Logan Douglas and Kalen Black.

Abby had been fighting the almost magnetic pull she felt to both men for years. She'd been a college student despite the fact she was only fifteen when she'd first met them. And much to her disappointment, they'd seen her as the young girl she'd been and not the mature woman she'd envisioned herself to be. Looking back on how she'd shamelessly flirted with all of her brother's friends, it was a wonder any of them had ever visited the ranch more than once. But she had learned some valuable lessons hanging around all those alpha males. They had taught her enough about self-defense to spark a lifetime interest. She still trained at least twice a week...more often if she could manage it. She also learned to speak her mind and think on her feet, because they had loved challenging her.

Jace had always been proud of her and had never made any secret of her advanced placement in school, so his friends had enjoyed sparring with her on any topic…no matter how obscure…they could come up with. It had only taken her a few minutes to figure out that their quoted statistics and "facts" were highly suspect at best and that she should question everything. Now, looking back on those late night discussions around the fire pit she knew they were trying to make sure she knew better than to just accept what someone was trying to spoon-feed her.

Abby had mentioned it to Jace one time and he'd laughed, "It's their twisted way of making sure you don't fall for every line of bull-shit someone tosses your way. Think of it as having lots of big brothers who are all trying to make sure you are safe from the predators they know are out there…because they are among the worst." They had both laughed, but she had always known there was a definite truth to his words.

Last week, Logan and Kalen had both asked her a hundred and one questions about what she had meant by her comments about coming home to escape alpha male bullshit. Technically her comments had been accurate, even if grossly understated. The man in question was actually the front for a group of men who hoped to profit…enormously…from her current project. When the Energy Consortium hadn't been able to hire her away from Garrett Oil, they'd sent in Sergio Fantella. Oh he'd swept her off her feet at first. He'd been charming and had obviously done his homework well because he'd known all of her interests and exploited his "knowledge" of them shamelessly.

It still embarrassed her that she'd been suckered so easily, *cripes*. Shaking off those memories she focused on the fact she had managed to avoid spilling the whole story to the two men she *least* wanted to share it with. Shivering as she pushed off the stone wall, she turned to walk back through the party. She wanted to dance with Jace before she made her excuses and disappeared. Suddenly the hair on the back of her nape stood on end. Never one to discount instinct she quickly darted her gaze around, paying particular attention to the shadows. It was the same feeling anytime Kalen Black or Logan Douglas were near…but that couldn't be it tonight because Jace had told her before the wedding they weren't going to make it back as planned. And while she'd been relieved to know she wouldn't have to dodge them all day and evening, there had been a small part of her that had been disappointed also.

Shaking her head at her own wayward thoughts, Abby made her way over to her brother and politely cut in on the elderly librarian who had been stepping all over his loafer-clad feet. "Bet that was fun, those dress shoes are no match for her orthopedic clodhoppers."

Jace chuckled, "True that, but her heart is in the right place even though I had to remove her hand from my ass more than once."

"Bet my new sister-in-law loved that."

"Oh, she is going to get a few swats for the giggling fit she had when she and Gage danced by me, don't think she won't." His words might have been harsh, but his tone was teasing. And while Abby knew that Holly was both Jace and Gage's submissive, she also recognized that both men were sap-happy in love with the woman. Both the Garrett and Hughes families had fallen in love with Holly as well. She was smart, driven, caring, and willing to take on their Dominant sons…what wasn't to love about that?

"She's wonderful, be nice to her…I wanna keep her around. She's good for you and think of the bragging rights I'll have now." Abby had teased her brother and bonus brother this past week unmercifully wondering what the talented writer and actress saw in the two of them.

"Be nice, Short Round, or I'll hand you over to the stalkers at the edge of the dance floor." When Abby tried to look, her brother had already anticipated her response and spun her around so that his large torso blocked her view. "Aw hell, I'm going to hand you off anyway because it's my turn to dance with Holly." He stopped and brushed his fingers down her cheek, "Sweetie, please give them a chance to help you with whatever sent you high-tailing it home. If you won't talk to me, please talk to them. Protecting people is what we do." He pulled her into a rib-crushing hug and then before she could even blink he turned her away from him and stalked away.

Blinking at his sudden movements and departure, Abby looked up to find herself face to chest with Kalen and Logan. And in an instant she found herself right back on the Bi-Polar Express…wishing they hadn't made it back and thrilled to find them standing in front of her.

* * * *

Kalen didn't even try to suppress his smile at the way her eyes widened in surprise and then desire. Nor did he miss the small gasp or the way the pulse at the base of her neck picked up. *Oh, love, your body knows something your mind has yet to accept.*

"Abigail, dance with me." He didn't ask—he wasn't going to give her a chance to say no. He watched her gulp and he saw the questions in her eyes.

Logan stepped forward and kissed her on the forehead, "We were delayed, sorry baby. You look gorgeous by the way. Now dance with Kalen, but the next one is mine." Logan stepped back and Kalen pulled her close and moved them smoothly around the small dance floor. The candlelight highlighted the golden tone of Abby's skin and gave it an almost ethereal appearance. The deep red gown she wore shimmered as the gold-tinted lights danced in its sheen. Kalen was just under six feet tall and even in the heels she was wearing, he still towered over her. And there was something about her that brought out every protective instinct he possessed. He had spent years studying the writings of the ancient mystics and had often wondered at their descriptions of *the one*. And even though he and Logan believed

Abby was their destiny, he was all too aware that they had a mountain of resistance ahead of them. She was going to fight them all the way—but her submission would be all the sweeter because of their struggle to earn it.

"I didn't think you were going to be here? I mean, Jace mentioned that you'd gone to help the ShadowDance team rescue a little girl and that you'd been delayed."

Kalen heard the sadness and disappointment in her comments even if she hadn't intended to share it. Leaning back he brushed his lips over hers and then spoke against her ear, "We tried to get back in time, love. But Boomer thought he had to rock western Costa Rica, so the natives were a bit restless. By the time we'd gotten alternate transportation, we were running way behind."

Abby pulled back and looked into his eyes, "The explosion in Costa Rica two days ago was you guys? Holy hell hath Hannah." Kalen had to laugh because her expression was something between shock and appreciation. "Wish I could have seen *that*." Well, he hadn't expected that reaction that was for sure.

"Well, that is why we call him Boomer. But a very sweet young girl is back in her family's loving care this evening so we'll call the mission a resounding success." It had also helped pull Logan further out of the hole he'd been in since his last mission with the Teams as well. Callie had been the beginning of his healing, their boss's new wife had been a spark of happiness on the small island that housed Club Isola and was now her new home. Just thinking about the little tigress that was now heading up Ian's resort brought a smile to his face. In many ways, Abby, Holly, and Callie were all similar—they were all three extremely bright and fiercely loyal—but Callie's and Holly's submission was instantly obvious to any Dom who met them. Abby's submission would have to be earned, slowly and with methodical precision.

When the song ended, Kalen held her in his arms for long moments just enjoying the feeling of her softness pressed against his strength. Holding her touched his soul and proved once again that the ancients had gotten it right when they'd written that peace might begin within one's self, but it was drawn to the surface by the magnetism of one's soul mate. Leaning down to brush his lips over hers again he felt her whole body shudder as he whispered, "There's more, so much more, if you'll just let us show you." Before she could answer, he turned her into Logan's waiting arms.

Chapter 24

Holly wasn't really sure her mind had caught up with the whirlwind that had suddenly become her life. She'd been crazy busy and stressed before, but this was nothing like the drain that had been. Now her life centered on the two men who had swept her up into a tidal wave of love and lust that just seemed to build every day. There didn't seem to be any end to their creative ways of showing her just how much they wanted her. Laughing to herself, she realized that if it hadn't been for all the help she'd had, the ceremonies and celebration she was now enjoying would have been a total bust.

Jace's mom, Beth Hughes, had done as much or more than Pilar Garrett…both women had worked tirelessly and called in their friends and family to help as well. Geez, the mountain of food they'd prepared would have probably fed a family of six for a month of Sundays. They had shooed her from the kitchen each and every time she'd tried to help until they'd finally threatened to tell her men if she didn't go and rest. Holly had to admit that the time she'd spent resting had helped her heal far more than she'd expected it to. She had even fired up her laptop for the first time a couple of days ago and had been thrilled with the creative energy that had seemed to flow from her like a bubbling fountain.

When she had missed a couple of meals because she'd been lost in her work, Gage and Jace had quickly explained that her priority was taking care of herself. She still shivered when she thought about how they'd explained precisely how severe the consequences would be for not taking good care of their *property*.

Holly had finally broken down and called her parents. After they'd both berated her for the negative publicity she'd received for her "accident" she'd wondered how they had managed to make the word sound like something a cat would try to bury. Both her mother and her father had told her to get back to work on the projects she had pending and reminded her that a lot of people depended on her finishing things on time. And they hadn't even tried to hide their disgust with fact that she worked for a man who owned a sex club which had made Holly wonder what her mother would say if she knew her best friend was a member of Ian's club, and she had barely resisted the urge to tell her. It was only the fact that club members' names were a closely guarded secret that had kept Holly from yanking the rug out from under her mother's carefully crafted world.

It had been liberating to realize that for the first time that Holly could remember, she hadn't been affected by either of her parents' negative opinions. She'd just been grateful that her parents were in Europe and hadn't been at all interested in returning to see their only child be married. Her mother had called her relationship with two men *distasteful* and *common* so Holly had sighed with relief when they hadn't mentioned attending.

When Jace had called Ian, Callie had been quite disgruntled knowing they couldn't get home from Thailand in time. The couple was enjoying an extended honeymoon and working their way through some of the world's most exotic locales. Jace had put Ian's feisty submissive on speaker phone and Holly had laughed when she'd finally quieted down at Ian's command and sniffed, "Well, okay, but their collaring ceremony is *mine*! I want full creative control and I have some wickedly wonderful ideas." Holly had laughed when all three men had groaned.

* * * *

Gage stood back watching as Holly seemed to be lost in memories—some good and some not so much so, judging from her changing expressions. He'd love to know where her mind was taking her. Discovering something new about her each and every day was his new favorite pastime. He had already danced with her several times and each time a little bit more of the wall she'd held herself behind for so many years fell away. Watching her blossom in their care was one of the most amazing things he'd ever witnessed.

They were leaving tomorrow for New York. He and Jace had agreed it was only fair that since they'd shown her all around their hometown that she should get to show them hers as well. He knew there would likely be media to deal with, but she'd insisted that was her parents' issue, not hers. Despite her assurances that they wouldn't be bothered, Gage's sixth sense had kicked in and he'd called Mitch Grayson to ask him to put out some feelers and see what was floating around in the journalistic cesspool of the gossip rags. What he'd learned hadn't helped his feelings of unease either. He hadn't had a chance to mention anything to Jace until a few minutes ago and from the tight line his friend's mouth had drawn into, Gage was guessing he was of the same opinion—they were walking into a cluster-fuck tomorrow.

Gage and Jace knew that Logan and Kalen had planned to stay on at the ranch for a few days to relax after the Costa Rican mission and to see what kind of information they could pry out of Short Round when there weren't so many options for her to distract herself. Unfortunately that was going to have to wait. Jace and Gage both felt they should take the men with them instead, and Gage dreaded the moment Holly figured out the change of plans. She wasn't going to miss the change and it was going to cast a dark cloud over her memories of today's celebration and he knew neither he nor Jace was looking forward to disappointing her.

As he watched his mom and aunts approach Holly, she smiled as they quickly engaged her in their conversation. He smiled when she suddenly seemed to become aware that she was being watched. When she slowly turned her face toward him, his heart nearly melted at the smile that lit her face. Damn it was an amazing feeling to have someone that delighted to see you. He crooked his finger in a come-here motion and smiled when she turned to the other women and said her goodbyes. The white dress she'd chosen for the wedding and commitment ceremonies flowed around her. The pattern of beads and small crystals sewn onto the dress made it shimmer and sparkle just like light dancing over moving water. When she had descended the stairs in the Garretts' home earlier today, he and Jace had both gasped. Sappy as it sounded, she had looked just like a princess in some fairy tale, and Gage knew that moment in time would forever be etched in his memory.

When she got close enough, he grabbed her delicate wrist and pulled her against his chest. "I love watching you walk to me, although I'd appreciate it even more if you were naked. But I'll get that soon enough. I love you." He'd spoken the last against her ear and then pressed his lips against the sensitive spot just below her ear, and smiled as he felt goose bumps race over her dewy skin. "Cold, sweetheart?" He knew she wouldn't miss the chuckle in his voice.

"No, although I should be since my loving husbands relieved me of my panties before this party even started." He laughed because they had done exactly that, and in front of several of their friends too. They'd made it look like they were after a high garter, but they had actually taken her white satin panties also. Jace had pocketed the garter and he'd kept the panties for himself.

"That we did, but you know the rules, baby. No panties unless Jace or I specifically give them to you, because they impede our access. And I notice you didn't mention that you are also wearing the last of the butt plugs, so you should be ready to take both of us tonight. Now, about that access—let me show you just how handy this is going to be." He took a couple of slow steps back into the shadows pulling her with him. He turned Holly so that her bare back was against his chest, Christ he loved this dress. The halter design was going to let him slip is hands inside to play with her tight nipples while he fucked her. Unsnapping his pants he quickly freed his throbbing cock and gave it a couple of quick strokes knowing she'd be able to feel his movements through the silky fabric separating her wonderfully bare ass and pussy from his movements.

He gathered up her dress and ran his fingers between her legs sliding his fingers over her smooth pussy. She and Abby had enjoyed a spa day as their treat a couple of days ago and they'd left the staff very specific instructions about waxing their fiancée. And they had been very pleased with the results, even though she'd sworn that next time she wanted the mimosas in advance. *Oh yeah, we'll make sure you keep everything just like this—nice and smooth.* "You're so wet for me wife. I can't tell you how happy that makes me." He used her slick syrup to rim her rear hole and smiled as she tried—unsuccessfully—to stifle her moan.

Sitting on a large smooth rock, Gage pulled her over his lap and quickly positioned his cock at her entrance and rocked his hips up until he was inside and then pulled her down until he was balls deep in ecstasy. "Oh my God, you are so huge inside me. And each ridge and bump...oh God...they light me up from the inside out." Her whispered words were sweet music to his ears as he let her fuck herself on his cock for a few strokes before he reached around her and slid his finger inside her dress to pinch her nipples.

This time her gasp wasn't quite as quiet and he wondered for just a minute if he should have turned her around so he'd be able to stifle her screams with his kiss. Then Gage noticed Jace slipping through the shadows, a smile lighting his face. As Jace stepped up in front of her, Gage saw him reaching for his belt and smiled. "Our wife is going to make a lot of noise when she comes and likely attract some unwanted attention, so I think I'll give her something to fill that pretty little mouth so she doesn't bring the Ladies Aide Society out in force. Damn, most of those women have cell phones that would make Ian envious, and if they know how to use the cameras we'll make the local paper and be on their Facebook pages by morning."

Gage would have laughed but he knew it was true because he'd seen several of them videotaping the ceremony. "True enough, give her something to distract her before she milks me to oblivion before I'm ready to end this."

Looking around Holly's bare shoulders, Gage watched Jace feed his cock into their wife's mouth. Gage could hear the strain in Jace's voice and he drew his fingers down the side of her sweet face and spoke to her, "That's a good girl, pet. Take me to the back of your— *oh shit*—throat and swallow. *Fuck me* that's perfect. Oh Jesus, Joseph, and Mary, that feels fantastic, love. When you hollow your cheeks as you pull back it sends lightning right up my spine."

Gage knew there were always going to be people who wouldn't understand their ménage relationship and that Holly would be the one to take the brunt of those narrow-minded comments because most people wouldn't mess with either he or Jace. One night about a year ago when they'd been talking about sharing, Jace had mentioned watching his dads comfort his mom after a man at the grocery store had made a snide remark to her.

Jace had told Gage that he'd been seventeen at the time and had met the young man at the back of the grocery store when he'd gotten off work that night. Even though Jace hadn't elaborated, it had been clear that Pilar Garrett's son had taken serious issue with the man's treatment of his sweet mama. Jace's fathers' approach had been more subtle, but just as effective. The next day they'd bought the store and promptly fired the young man.

There would be hurdles he knew, but he also knew that she was going to be worth each and every one of them. Protecting Holly was always going to be their number one priority, and unfortunately, Gage had a feeling they were going to get a crash course in media management sooner rather than later.

But right now, he wanted to give her the experience they'd all been waiting for. Before she could go over the edge of release and take both he and Jace with her on the ride, he slid out of her and pulled the plug from her ass at the same time. Luckily Jace hadn't pulled his cock from her mouth yet because her groan of frustration would have been recognized by every Dom at the party.

Gage quickly shifted his hips so that the head of his cock was pressed against her rosette. "Are you ready to be fucked by both of your Masters at the same time, sweetness?" She didn't even try to answer, but she thrust her hips back in a sharp move that sent him past the tight right of muscles and sensitive nerves encircling her ass and he wanted to paddle her for the risk she'd taken. "Fuck me. You deserve a paddling for that move baby. But you feel so fucking good I can't think of anything else right now."

Jace pulled from her mouth and stepped forward and lifted her dress and pulled her legs up so that his arms were under her knees. Gage saw him smile down at her, "I'm letting my mind take a mental picture of the moonlight shining down on your passion-filled eyes. Your lips are swollen from sucking my cock and everything about this moment is absolutely perfect."

Gage was already fully seated in her ass and he could feel Jace pressing in through the thin membrane separating them. Knowing they were about to share their wife for the very first time sent a wave of emotion cresting through Gage that had almost blindsided him. Once Jace was balls deep they began alternating their strokes. As Jace pulled back, Gage pressed in deep. They were going to have to make this short and sweet because their lovely bride had already been on the brink of release and they probably didn't have a lot of time before they were interrupted.

Gage leaned further back and reached around Holly so he could roll and pinch her tight nipples as he pulled her back against his chest. The move gave Jace enough room to slide his hand between them and Gage knew immediately when Jace pinched her clit because she clamped down on his cock like a vise. Gage could see Jace lean down and brush his lips over hers and from her gasp he knew that small shift was causing Jace's cock to press against her G-spot with each stroke.

Holly's entire body stiffened and Gage felt her ass and vaginal muscles begin rippling. At Jace's almost imperceptible nod they both pushed deep at the same time. And just as Jace crushed his mouth against hers Gage spoke against her ear, "Come for us, sweetness." Her response was immediate and cataclysmic. Gage knew she'd screamed and was grateful Jace had caught it in their kiss because that was the only thing that had kept her pleasure from being heard in the next county. Gage didn't need to hear Jace's groan to know he'd found his release as well, because he'd been able to feel the pulses of Jace's seed that were bathing her cervix. Hell, he'd had to bite down on her shoulder to muffle his own growl as Holly's tight little ass had milked him dry. "Un-fucking-believable. Sweetheart, you are amazing." It took him another couple of seconds to draw in enough oxygen to speak again. Jace had already pulled back and was whispering sweet words to her as Gage pulled free and used a handkerchief to clean both.

Once Gage had set their clothing to rights, he stood up and took Holly into his arms. While he was holding her, he noticed Logan had been standing with his back to them, but their friend was blocking the path that would have led anyone curious about their disappearance right to them. *Damn, you have to love friends that always have your back.*

Chapter 25

As expected, Holly had started asking questions the minute she'd heard Kalen and Logan were accompanying them to New York. Their sweet wife hadn't been a happy camper when she found out they had known last night about the fact the media had already been alerted that she'd married two men and that they were already staking out the airports in and around the city. Jace could tell that Holly had held her tongue even when he'd been convinced steam was about to erupt from her diamond studded ears.

Jace had gotten up early, leaving Holly snuggled in bed with Gage so that he could talk with Abby before they left. He had barely gotten to speak with her alone and he wanted to apologize for taking Logan and Kalen when he was sure his little sister had been looking forward to a little fun and games before she had to return to work next week.

He'd found Abby sitting with her legs curled under her on one of the loungers by the pool. She was sipping her coffee and he knew without even asking that she'd added several scoops of mocha mix making it the caffeine equivalent of an H-bomb. Settling down across from her, he saw the dark circles under her eyes indicating she wasn't sleeping well and he wondered when she was going to let someone help with whatever problem she was running from. "Short Round, I'm sorry I haven't spent more time with you this trip. I feel like I've let you down and I'm afraid I'm about to make it worse."

Jace saw her hands tense around the mug she was holding and the small frown that wrinkled between her brows. "I know you've been busy, Indy, no worries. But what's up that you think you're going to make my life more difficult? Good luck with that by the way." Her chuckle lacked sincerity and he inwardly flinched.

"Recent intel indicates a media ambush for Holly when she arrives back in New York today. Evidently someone locally posted details of our marriage online and the vultures have been alerted and are circling. I'm not too sure that her mom's best friend and her father's agent aren't involved as well." He shook his head at the fact that her family counted those people as friends. "We're pulling Kalen and Logan in as backup, they'll be heading back with us instead of staying here for a few days." The flash of disappointment in her eyes was masked so quickly that if he hadn't been watching carefully, he'd have missed it. *Fuck I hate disappointing her.*

"Not to worry, big brother mine. It's about time for me to get back to work anyway." The slight wobble in her voice gave her away even if she'd masked her response in record time.

"Abby, I don't know what's happening, and I'm only going to say this once, I promise you—but it's important to me so listen up little sister. I love you and there isn't anything I won't do to help you, but you have to let me in. And if you won't ask me for help, please ask someone." He gave her a tight smile before adding, "And I have some pretty narrow parameters on who I think you should ask, but I think that goes without saying."

She shifted in her seat and after several long minutes of silence she finally looked up at him and nodded. "I've missed you, Indy. Maybe I'll come visit you after you've settled in. Might be getting close to time for a change or two in my life anyway." She finally took a deep breath and a bright smile lit her face for the first time since they'd been talking, "When are you and my bonus brother going to make me an aunt?"

Jace leaned his head back and laughed, "Damn, Short Round, mom put you up to that? Hell, she and the dads are already planning a nursery for one of the upstairs bedrooms." And Jace knew that Gage had heard similar comments from his own family. Seems when you wait until after you're thirty to get married your parents are a bit impatient for their grandchildren to make an appearance."

"Nope, I was bright enough to come up with it all on my own." Her grin told him she was kidding—or at least mostly kidding. Damn he'd missed her more than he'd ever thought possible and suddenly his heart felt a small emptiness that only family can fill. *Well hell, I haven't even left yet and I'm already starting to get homesick.*

* * * *

Their flight to New York had been an exercise in frustration and it hadn't taken Holly long to figure out that soldiers were accustomed to much more efficient methods of transportation. And when those soldiers worked for billionaires with their own jets they were even more impatient…oh and add in the fact they were all Doms? Hell, she wasn't even going to go there. They had surrounded her the minute they had disembarked at JFK and she had been jogging to keep up with their long strides all the way through the crowded terminal. She had just opened her mouth to tell them that she was tired of running and their information had obviously been flawed when she was blinded by what seemed like a thousand cameras flashing from all directions as they exited the secure area of the airport.

"God damn it." Jace's curse was pitched low but she hadn't missed the frustration in his tone. He and Gage had flanked her with Kalen leading them and Logan following. And she'd thought they were moving quickly before, but now they were jogging which left her to run and she *hated running*.

"Hey, guys? I can't…I ugh…keep up. You have to slow down." She was already panting and her new husbands looked at her as if she'd just sprouted a second head. "Don't give me that look. I'm overweight and out of shape, so sue me." Okay, so that wasn't probably the wisest choice of words, but damn she was about to expire here.

Without even slowing his pace, Jace scooped her up in his arms and growled in her ear, "That's five swats, pet. Now bury your face in my shoulder until we settle you in the back of the limo." His words shouldn't have caused her pussy to clench and then flood, but they did. For some reason her body was totally on board with being a submissive…it was just her mouth that hadn't seemed to get the memo yet.

Once she'd been pushed through the door of the waiting limo she'd been surprised to see Gage and Jace hand their luggage claim tickets to Kalen and Logan. The other men turned back to the entrance to the baggage claim area as Gage and Jace climbed in beside her and the limo sped away from the curb. "Hey, what about Kalen and Logan? Aren't we going to wait for them? How are they going to get to the hotel? We can't just leave them."

Gage shook his head and smiled, "Baby, they have fast-roped in the dead of night into some of the most dangerous places on the earth. I think they can handle picking up our luggage and hailing a cab." Well, that made sense and now that she thought about it she felt pretty silly and knew her cheeks were flushing with her embarrassment. "And I have to say, you should really be glad they aren't along for this ride because I do believe you have a punishment coming for that crack about being overweight."

She felt her whole body flush with arousal and knew they wouldn't miss the increase in her breathing either. Hell, as loud as the blood sounded rushing in her ears, they could probably hear it too. "What? It's true…I was only—" Her words were cut off by their raised brows. *Damn, what did they do rehearse that so they were in perfect synch?* Suddenly the sundress she'd chosen to wear didn't seem like such a wise choice, particularly when she remembered the thong she was wearing despite their instructions to go without underwear unless one of them had specifically given it to her. *Oh frack.*

Gage's smile didn't reach his eyes as he considered her, "Just now remembered that thong you didn't think we knew you were wearing, didn't you?" She hadn't been able to smother her gasp of surprise and the rat had the audacity to laugh at her reaction. "Baby, you are going to learn quickly that fooling your Dom is going to be not only virtually impossible, but also very unwise."

Gage held out his hand, "Give me the panties, sweetness." When she only blinked as if he'd been speaking some foreign language, he simply said, "*Now,*" and something in her subconscious snapped and she scrambled to raise her dress without flashing them and peeled the tiny triangle of pink satin down her legs and then laid them in his up-turned palm. "Good girl, now over my lap, sweetheart. I'll give you five for the panties before Jace gives you his five for that self-deprecating and very inaccurate comment." He paused and she nervously shot her gaze toward the window where the driver would have a clear view of her bare ass if she laid over his knees.

"Your job is to obey, not think or worry about what someone else can see." Gage's fingers grasped her chin forcing her to focus on his handsome face. "Trust us to never put you in danger, sweetheart."

She nodded and felt tears fill her eyes and they hadn't even punished her yet, but just knowing that she'd disappointed them sent a stab of pain through her heart. She took a steadying breath and slowly draped herself over his lap. He easily repositioned her so that her ass was peaked and she knew it was exactly in line with his palm. He was kneading her ass cheeks through the thin cotton of her sundress and just as she thought maybe he would spank her through the dress, he slowly raised it so that her ass was bare to the world.

The first swat was sharp and it not only hurt more than she had expected, but it also surprised her enough that she couldn't help her squeak. *Holy shit that hurt. Hell, I'm not sure I can take nine more of those. What are his damned hands made of...cast iron skillets?*

"Tell me why you are being punished, sweetness." She could hear the gravelly tone of his voice, but she wasn't sure if it was from frustration or desire.

"Panties…um, I wore panties when neither of you gave them to me, Sir." Her words were immediately followed by three more stinging slaps and her ass felt like it was on fire.

Gage kept his hand over the places he'd swatted and his hand kept the heat in and made everything inside her sizzle. She was just about to move when she realized his fingers were trailing down the crack of her ass, but before she could voice a protest he leaned over her and said, "Open your legs for me." She hesitated because she knew he what he was going to find…she was soaking wet. Good God how could she be aroused at having her bare ass set aflame as if she was an errant child. When he pushed his fingers through her dripping sex her whole body went on alert. Damn, if he would just slide his fingers a couple of inches further, he would brush her aching clit and that would be enough to push her over the edge.

Her brain was so muddled with desire that for a few seconds she'd forgotten he had one slap to go and just as he raised his hand to deliver the last blow, she realized her pussy was totally exposed. But before she could react she felt his hand connect with the tender engorged tissues of her labia. *Oh my fucking God, my pussy is on fire and not in a good way.* Holly felt the sob well up from deep inside her and heard herself scream. "Don't make me punish you for this ever again, baby. Your Masters want easy access to what is theirs—and this lovely cunt belongs to us. Remember the swats will double each time, so I suggest you remember this lesson."

Holly suddenly realized that she was sitting on his lap and sobbing into his shoulder. *When did he sit me up?* "I'm so sorry. It just seemed wrong to go out in public with my private bits bare." Between gasping breaths, she finally managed to add, "But mostly I'm sorry I disappointed you."

Chapter 26

Jace had watched as Gage gave Holly the first four swats and he knew the fifth one was going to hurt like hell, but she had certainly earned it by wearing the panties despite their very specific instructions not to. He'd been glad that their driver was actually a member of the McGregor Holdings security team. Tony Dent had been a Navy SEAL until shrapnel from a roadside bomb cost him most of his left leg. At six foot three with the body of a man dedicated to his recovery he was the poster child for the power of physical therapy. Tony had taken to the prosthesis he'd agreed to test for Uncle Sam and had quickly beaten every trainee on base in both sprints and longer runs with full gear and packs, but he'd still been told he couldn't return to active duty and opted out rather than take a desk job.

Jace had been more than happy to have him on board and had specifically requested him for this assignment. Tony's confidence had flagged a bit after leaving the teams and Jace knew that if he and Gage showed him that they trusted him to help protect their new wife, Tony would understand that their protestations of confidence weren't empty platitudes. Glancing up Jace caught Tony's small smile in the rearview mirror. Every Dom appreciated the value of a sub's vulnerability after a punishment scene and the experienced ones also understood the importance of aftercare that was tailored to meet the sub's needs.

Jace had known subs that wanted cuddling and those who wanted to be left completely alone, and all shades in between. He had personally never been big on being openly affectionate in public until he'd spent time with Callie McGregor. Jace had teased her often telling her that she'd taught him as much or more than he'd taught her, and in many ways it was true. Holly reminded Jace of Callie in many ways, including her innate understanding of the healing power of touch.

Deciding that it was time to proceed he signaled Gage and waited while he turned her so that she faced him. Jace made an effort to keep his tone modulated as he spoke to her, "Pet, tell me what you did that earned you the five strokes you'll be getting at my hand." Her big green eyes were still shiny from her tears and she had suddenly become very interested in her fingers as they twisted the soft fabric of her dress in her lap. "I asked you a question, pet, and I expect an answer. You might want to think about how close we are to your apartment. Do you really want the doorman standing by the open door while you get the last of your punishment?"

He saw her sharp intake of breath and the trembling in her hands wasn't the good kind that indicated a hidden desire for voyeurism either. "No, oh please don't do that...I can't even tell you how horrible that would be. You're going to punish me for saying I was too heavy, and I know you don't like hearing me say it, but when you meet my mother you'll understand. I want to unlearn it, but it isn't going to happen overnight....I'm sorry." Her last words were little more than a whisper, but he hadn't missed the fact that she obviously felt torn. On the one hand was the negative self-image that had been all she'd known growing up, and on the other, was the very sudden and new expectations of the two Dominant men she'd just married.

He leaned forward and drew his knuckles down her tear streaked cheek, "We love you, pet, and we want you to see how much we value you as well. Your curves are perfect, your heart is huge and giving, and you're smart with a wicked sense of humor when you feel safe enough to let it show. We plan on cherishing you for the rest of our lives and a part of that is teaching you to love and respect yourself." Her tears were falling freely again and he knew that as deeply as her submission ran, she was berating herself for disappointing them and that she would continue down that path until she felt like she had atoned for her behavior. His punishment would hurt, but it would also free her from the guilt she was carrying.

"Lay over my knees, pet. Let's get this over with so it's behind us and you can let it go." She put herself in the same position Gage had put her in and he could feel her tensing. "Don't tense up your muscles or it will hurt more than it should. Spread your legs a bit." When she parted her thighs, he ran his fingers through her sweet honey and was pleased to find her soaking wet. Gage's last swat to her bare pussy hadn't been enough to thwart her arousal and he was enormously pleased by that.

Usually it was Gage that gave the harsher spanking, but this time it would be Jace and he suddenly understood why Ian had so often gone easy on Callie—damn it was going to be hard to give her the swats she needed. He plunged his fingers into her sheath and fucked her several strokes with his fingers before curving them up so that he brushed her G-spot. When he felt her starting to tremble, he pulled his fingers back and smiled up at Gage when she moaned at the loss.

Giving her four very harsh swats on alternating ass cheeks he found no satisfaction in her sobs. Leaning over her he pushed his fingers back inside her and brought her right back up to the top again. "Remember this lesson, pet. I don't want to repeat it and you don't want that either because your ass is already flaming red or hot to the touch." He made sure his callused fingertips were brushing over the tiny bundle of nerves that he knew would send her right over the top and just as he knew she was nearing the point of no return he leaned over and whispered close to her ear, "As soon as the last swat hits your beautiful ass, I want you to come for me." And just as he spoke the words he withdrew his fingers from her heat and gave her a hard slap right over the center of her burning ass so that the sting would have hit her pussy lips as well. Just as she screamed at the pain, he plunged his fingers back in deep and she came immediately. The fresh wave of honey that coated his fingers was almost enough to pull him right over the edge of that cliff with her.

Twisting his fingers around so that he could keep her riding the wave of her release as long as possible, Jace was lost in the moment as if he had come right along with her, until he heard her whispered chant, "I'm so sorry...so sorry. Please don't send me away. I'll do better, I promise...please give me another chance."

What the fuck? Is she serious? Looking up at Gage he could see the confusion in his eyes and knew that look probably mirrored his own baffled expression. Jace pulled her up onto his lap quickly and bracketed her small face with his large hands. When she wouldn't meet his gaze, he spoke firmly, "Holly, look at me right now." Her hiccupped sobs didn't seem to be easing much but when she finally looked up at him, he was nearly leveled by the look of devastation in her eyes. Obviously he and Gage were going to have to do some major work on her self-esteem and it didn't appear that punishment spankings were going to be the answer. "Holly, do you really think that our love is so weak that it would fail this easily? Because baby, I have to tell you, there isn't anything you that you can do to shake what we feel for you. Just because our love hasn't been tested by time doesn't mean it's not going to endure. And our disappointment in your lack of self-esteem is because we know it's so unfounded."

Pulling her against his chest he was almost overcome with guilt. She had taken her punishment from Gage without incident because she had known that she had *earned it* by choosing to disobey their instructions. But *his* punishment had been devastating to her because he'd been punishing her for something that was actually her parents' responsibility. To know that for the first time in years he'd really let a sub down was like a kick in the gut. But knowing he'd hurt the most important person in his life sent an arrow of pain-laced guilt straight through his heart.

"Pet, I hope you can forgive me." Jace didn't miss Holly's quiet inhalation at his words and when she pulled back so she could meet his gaze he smiled at her and kissed the end of her nose. "Don't look so surprised, sweet wife. Doms make mistakes too and I hope that when it happens, Master Gage and I will both be wise enough to admit it, apologize, and hope you'll forgive us." Jace had seen both of his fathers apologize to his mother more than once and he knew the power of admitting when you were wrong.

"I understand…well, I think I do. You feel bad for punishing me for believing the garbage my parents taught me, don't you?" Jace had never met a woman as intuitive and tuned in to him as Holly was. "Can we just put this behind us and move on? I'm nervous about what we're going to find at my apartment, and I know we are all tired from traveling. I hate being ambushed by reporters. And I swear to you, if I find out my father's agent is behind this…that he is using me to garner attention for the movie he has coming out next week, I'm going to be one wicked woman."

Jace laughed and heard Gage chuckle as well, "Well, my love, we'll let you steamroll your family and the agent, but you have to promise us two things. First, you'll leave enough for Master Gage and me to tear a strip off their hides as well, and second, you'll defer to us on any issue that involves your personal safety—*always.*" His heart warmed when she dropped her eyes and slowly nodded her agreement.

Glancing up at Gage, Jace watched as he shook his head back and forth grinning. Jace knew exactly what was going through his friend's mind and he agreed—hell no she wasn't anywhere near ready to concede all that control to them yet, but he knew it would come in time. She'd lived on her own and built not one, but several different successful careers for herself, so she had independence and self-sufficiency deeply ingrained in her psyche. But with time, trust, and a firm hand, Jace was sure he and Gage were going to be able to help her see the benefit of letting them shoulder some of the burden for her. But those were issues for another day, right now, they needed to concentrate on getting her safely into her apartment and judging from the small mob surrounding the front door that didn't look like it was going to be all that easy.

Jace continued to hold Holly and tried to distract her while Gage conferred with Tony about alternate entrances into the building. After driving through the parking garage and finding more reporters at that entrance, Jace decided that even though they would have to walk through the crazies from that nut-case church in Kansas, they were counting on the presence of television cameras to keep anyone from doing anything over the top.

As they pulled up to the curb, Jace set Holly on the seat next to him and helped her straighten her clothing and smiled as she dabbed on lipstick and tried to finger comb her hair. "Pet, you are a newlywed in a ménage relationship emerging from the back of a limo—trust me, everyone is going to be expecting you to look like you have been enjoying the ride." He waggled his eyebrows at her and for just a few seconds he wasn't sure she was going to find any humor in his antics. But she finally broke out in a smile that Jace was convinced could have lit up half the city. Then she burst out laughing and threw her arms around his neck and hugged him tightly.

"Thank you for knowing how much I needed that laugh, Master." Jace felt his heart swell with her impromptu hug and the way the title of Master had rolled so easily off her tongue. He wanted to tell her that he and Gage planned to always know just what she needed, but limo door opened and they were immediately besieged by shouted questions and the blinding flashes of every conceivable type of recording device known to man. Christ, Jace truly believed facing armed enemy soldiers was easier than these lunatics with their flashing cameras and screaming tirades. And through the din of people shouting questions and comments that were intended to spark a reaction that would then be splashed across the front page of every newspaper in the free world, Jace heard a man shout, "Die heathen," and the unmistakable sound of a small hand gun being fired at close range just before Holly sagged in his arms.

Chapter 27

Holly felt like she was floating and she wondered why everyone in the distance was yelling and why she was suddenly gasping for breath. Had she been working out? For several seconds she just tried to concentrate on remembering what she'd been doing. Suddenly she realized she was in Jace's arms and he was running, and the memory of walking through the crowd came back like a strong breeze pushing away the fog of a fall morning at her parents' country estate. But why did her side ache and it seemed like she couldn't take a deep breath and her need for oxygen was quickly trumping every other thought wafting through her confusion.

Jace must have sensed her struggle because he spoke quietly to her, "Hang on pet, EMS has an ETA of less than a minute now and they'll have everything we need to make it easier for you to breathe. Right now what Gage and I need is for you to stay just as calm as possible, can you do that for us, love? Don't try to talk, just nod your head if you understand." Holly was grateful that she didn't have to answer because she wasn't sure she would have been willing to give up the small amount of air she was getting in order to form the words. When she merely nodded he looked down at her and smiled. It was only then that she realized he'd stopped and that they were surrounded by huge men.

Jace had to have seen the panic in her eyes because he immediately soothed her with a kiss to her forehead, "Holly, I'll be happy to introduce you to our team later, but for now, just know they are here to protect you—with their lives if necessary. And Gage will be joining us shortly, he has the shooter and if there is anything left of the bastard when he's done, then he'll turn the bastard over to the authorities. He'll join us the instant he can, I promise you." Somewhere in the back of her mind Holly realized she was being lowered onto a flat surface and someone put a mask over her face. As the sounds of sirens invaded the fog that was surrounding her, Holly decided to give in to the temptation of the darkness that kept trying to pull her under.

* * * *

Gage had seen the scrawny, older man draw a weapon just as he'd shouted his vile words at Holly. They had been surrounded by people and even if Gage had drawn a weapon he wouldn't have been able to get a shot off in time to stop the bullet that the self-righteous bastard had fired at Holly. Gage had known he had to stay and deal with the fruitcake, but watching Jace carry away their wife as he heard her gasping for breath had been the hardest thing he had ever done.

It had taken forever to complete the police reports and he'd been almost ready to pull his hair out by the time he'd been allowed to go to the hospital where they had taken Holly. After snarling at anyone who didn't move or answer his questions immediately, Gage finally opened the door to Holly's room and felt like his knees were going to fold. *Christ, can they hook her up to anything else?*

Jace met him at the door and moved him back into the hallway, "Damn, Hughes, I thought you were gonna drop in there. Come on, there is a small waiting room right down the hall." When he hesitated, Jace added, "Ian and Callie are with her and Daphne will back in a few minutes so she isn't alone."

Once they'd gotten to the waiting room, Jace leaned against the door while Gage took several breaths to regain his bearings. "Fuck me. I've seen a lot of bad shit—hell, we've both seen men die in the most gruesome ways imaginable—but that." All he could do was shake his head.

"It's a lot different when it's the woman you love, isn't it? Don't feel bad for caring. Hell, I probably would have lost it myself if Ian hadn't been by my side. I'm sorry I didn't meet you outside the door to warn you." Jace blew out a breath and then smiled tentatively, "The upside is that she is going to be fine. It was a through and through shot that chipped a rib, and it was that piece that hit her lung. The surgery to repair it was quick—well, once Ian arranged for the best surgical team from another hospital to be flown across the city."

Gage was just staring at him, trying to absorb and process the words. *She's really going to be fine? But she looked as white as the sheet that she was lying on.* "He wouldn't let them transfer her, right?"

"Got it in one. Hell, our usually unflappable boss was on a tear to get the best team over here and not one single fool tried to get in his way. The one nurse who even started to challenge him was backed right out of the room by Callie shaking her finger at the old bitty. Daphne has been handling the press but she's struggling to keep a lot of balls in the air at the same time." Jace knew he was throwing a lot of information at Gage in a short amount of time, but he also knew the man wouldn't rest until he was up to speed on everything he'd missed. "But I'm telling you, if Holly's wicked-assed mother or self-absorbed father call one more time, I'm not going to be responsible for my actions. I don't think there is any doubt that the agent tipped the press off that Holly would be arriving with both of her husbands, the only question is how much her parents knew and when. What's the story on the shooter?"

Gage took another deep breath and then explained that the man was the head of a group of crazies from a radical church in Kansas. They had already been in the city for another protest when they'd heard about Holly's polyamorous marriage. Gage explained that evidently the old guy felt safe because his daughter is a well-known lawyer who had him bonded out before the detectives had even finished with Jace. From what he'd heard, they old lunatic had recently been diagnosed with inoperable cancer so he didn't feel like he had anything to lose. If Gage had to guess, he'd bet the man's daughter had gotten her dad on a plane to God only knew where within the hour.

"She's really going to be alright? Damn, she was so pale. And could they hook her up to anything else?"

"Yeah, I talked to the surgeon and also listened while he was grilled by Daphne, Ian and Callie. The man is solid and didn't miss a beat in answering all of our questions. He's staying the night in the room next to Holly at Ian's *request*. As it turns out, the good doc has an interest in all things BDSM and Ian has given him a free lifetime membership. I think you'll actually like him once you meet him someplace else." Jace knew about Gage's dislike for hospitals, he'd never been in one to see someone who came out of it alive so Jace knew Gage worked hard to avoid them. But truthfully, Jace had never met a soldier yet who liked hospitals.

Nodding his head in reluctant acceptance, Gage looked at Jace, "We fucked up. We almost lost her because we didn't see it coming. I'm not sure I'll ever be able to forgive myself for this."

"Don't let Callie hear you say that. I said almost those exact same words and had my ass handed to me by Ian's little *Carlin*. Reminded me of why he nicknamed her 'little champion' to begin with. I'm telling you the woman's mouth is lethal sometimes. I'd like to think Ian will paddle her ass for the tongue lashing she gave me, but judging from his grin, I'm not all that hopeful." For the first time in several hours Gage felt as if the steel bands that had been tightening around his chest were loosening a bit. If his friend was joking around, then their woman must be alright.

"That's not to say I don't feel bad about what happened, but as Callie so clearly pointed out, we didn't have any way to know that crazy bastard was even in New York, let alone that he would target Holly." Jace let out a sigh that told Gage they were both at the seventh level of exhaustion hell. "Let's get back in there. I just wanted to update you where we wouldn't disturb her. But she was asking for you after they brought her back from surgery, and I'm not sure any of us managed to convince her that you hadn't been shot also. And she was convinced it was her fault because of the media circus that so often surrounds her."

Gage was speechless. *What the fuck! How could she possibly have known?* And in that moment he understood exactly what Callie had been trying to impress upon Jace. There wasn't any way any of them could have known. And now every priority they had shifted, and the only thing that mattered was healing Holly.

Chapter 28

Six weeks later

Holly paced the floor of the apartment her husbands had kept her sequestered in for the past month. The first two weeks after she'd been shot had been a blur thanks to some heavy medication. Holly had secretly named the nurse her husbands had hired to assist with her recovery Nurse Nancy the Nazi, because she had made sure Holly had taken her pain meds on time, even when she had begged to skip them so she could spend a little quality time with her laptop. And worse, the old bat had ratted her out to Jace and Gage. Both of her Masters had assured her they were keeping a tab on all of her infractions and that they intended to serve up each and every punishment she was due as soon as she was cleared by Dr. Donnie Dark.

Okay, so her doctor's name was actually Dr. Donald Whiteside, but that didn't sound nearly as appropriate after Holly learned that the trauma surgeon Ian had flown across the city was a Dom with some serious kinks and now had lifetime membership to Club Isola. She'd seen the good Doctor today at his new office in Alexandria and had gotten the all-clear to resume *normal* activities. The doctor's smug grin had let Holly know that he had probably already told her husbands she was cleared before he'd even told her…*the rat bastard*.

This morning before she'd left for her appointment, she'd begged her Masters to let her wear panties, but they had steadfastly refused. They'd been crystal clear about the consequences she would face if she decided to defy them and assured her that they would indeed know. *No doubt Dr. Donnie Dark would snitch me out in a heartbeat.*

After Gage had picked her up from her appointment he'd made her pull up her dress so that her bare ass and pussy were on a soft towel he'd placed on the seat and then he'd made her spread her legs wide and lift the front of her skirt so that he had a clear view of her freshly waxed mound. She'd been mortified that someone was going to see her until she remembered how darkly the windows were tinted and that he'd never but put her in danger, even if that danger was only to her reputation.

Both of her husbands were so in tune with her that she should have known her reaction wouldn't fly under Gage's radar. "I see you have worked this all out in your head, sweetness. I'm proud of you for thinking it all through before you questioned me, and I intend to reward you for that once we've gotten on the boat for the island." *Yep, that would have been panty soaking moment right there if she'd been wearing any.* She'd been waiting forever to be cleared by the doctor and would probably come the minute he touched her.

The boat ride to the island hadn't been nearly long enough in Holly's opinion. Gage had made her stand against the high rail with her legs spread wide and he'd used his fingers to bring her up to just shy of orgasm several times before he'd let her come. Jace had been standing on the dock to greet them and had smiled as she screamed her release just as they docked. It had taken her long minutes to recover enough to walk off the boat under her own power. Kalen Black had been at the luxurious boat's controls and he'd smiled at her as she'd walked unsteadily off the large deck. "Very nice, Holly. I'll be looking forward to your first scene at the club." The twinkle in his eye had caused her face to heat up so much she was sure it would have glowed in the dark.

Jace and Gage had brought her to the apartment and left her with instructions to rest, because as they'd said, she "was going to need it." But their promise had only served to rocket her arousal right back up until the nervous energy was almost pulsing out of her in waves of heated desire. She had tried to lie down, but that hadn't lasted any time at all. And now, she was pacing the width of the large living room. It wasn't exactly productive or restful, but Holly was much too antsy to sit still.

* * * *

Jace leaned back in his chair and looked at the security monitor and smiled. Oh his wife was nervous all right, and with good reason. She hadn't mentioned a very important incident that had occurred during her doctor's appointment today. Granted she had basically been set up to fail, but they were still going to enjoy the hell out of her first public scene tonight at the club.

Thank God Holly had signed the forms for both of her husbands to have unlimited access to her medical information, so their inquiry about her appointment today had yielded a lot of valuable information. Hell, it wasn't that Don wouldn't have shared the information anyway, because the code between Doms was more powerful than the privacy concerns for submissives in their care. And when it came to the health and safety of a sub, all restrictions were off—a fact their little angel was about to learn about firsthand.

Jace watched another monitor as Callie made her way down the hallway toward their apartment. She was so cute—her rounded belly such a contrast to her tiny frame. She looked like she'd tucked a ball under her shirt and from the back you'd never know the woman was even pregnant. He chuckled as Ian's sweet wife darted glances around as if she were trying to fly under their security radar—hell, she of all people ought to know it wasn't possible. When Holly had admitted her to the apartment he cranked up the sound and sent a quick text to Gage.

Callie's voice was clear even though she was trying to speak quietly when Holly opened the door without checking the security monitor first. *There's another five swats my love.* "Hey girlfriend, I just wanted to stop by and chitchat for a bit." Jace laughed out loud because Callie was just about the worst liar in the entire world. If Holly didn't know that was as piss-poor as excuses came, then she just wasn't paying attention.

He and Gage listened as the two women discussed all the usual topics women like to talk to death when Callie finally asked Holly, "Are you sure you are ready for tonight?" *Damn, how did Callie get wind of what they'd planned? No doubt about it, Ian's little sub has her nose to the ground.* Looking to his right, he almost laughed at Gage's "what the fuck" expression.

"Well, fuck me. How did she find out?" Gage's words echoed Jace's own question.

"No clue, but she has obviously charmed somebody and their ass is mine when I find out who it was. And Ian ought to paddle Callie's ass for this." Jace blew out a breath because he knew full well, Ian wasn't going to lay a hand on his pregnant wife. Jace had noticed Callie was becoming brattier by the day, and he was fairly sure it was her way of trying to get Ian's attention. Callie was a sub of the first order, and she craved her Dom's attention and his discipline. The sub inside Callie was trying to tell Ian that she missed the comfort and security she found in his Domination. Jace made a mental note to talk with Ian before the club opened this evening.

Holly looked slightly taken aback, "Oh shit, I don't know, now. What's going on? Oh dear, this explains the anxiety I've been feeling all day."

"No...I didn't mean anything bad is going to happen...although with your Masters who knows...but at least they haven't forgotten that you are their sub." Jace watched his sweet friend's shoulders sag and felt his heart tighten with the pain he saw on her face. Grabbing his phone he sent a quick text to Ian. "I just meant that it's going to be your first night at the club as a submissive and I wanted to make sure you are prepared for the things you are going to see and hear. It's a bit overwhelming if you aren't ready, and I didn't want you to have the same *issues* I had."

Holly raised her eyebrow in question, but Callie just forged ahead, "It's a long story and some evening after I have this baby we'll have a gab session over frozen margaritas and I'll tell you all about it, but I don't have a lot of time now. This place is wired for sight and sound and I'm sure your Doms already know I'm here, which means I'm already in trouble…hopefully. But I was worried for you and wanted to make sure your head is in the right place tonight." Callie took a deep breath and then smiled, "Yeah, I know, I know. Everybody gives me that look and no I don't know how I can say so much without stopping for a breath." Callie's laugh rang through the room and Jace was happy to see her smile and even more pleased to see a look of relief wash over Holly's sweet face.

Gage shook his head and chuckled, "God, you have to love Callie." Jace couldn't agree more. He'd worried that she was going to spoil all of their plans when she had just been trying to be a friend to Holly, and it endeared her to him even more.

Callie grasped Holly's hand in her own and smiled, "There will be a lot of people there tonight and things can get pretty intense. If you get scared, no matter how insignificant you think your fear is, tell one or both of your Masters. And if you can't for some reason, find me and I'll help. Also…and I can't even begin to tell you how important this is…remember to keep your focus on your Masters. I don't know what they have planned for you tonight, although I have a few guesses, but keep the fact that you trust them first and foremost in your heart and mind. Make certain all of your attention is on them and remind yourself frequently that they can only Dominate you if you submit."

Jace smiled at Holly's confused expression, damn she was so cute when she was perplexed over something. Callie smiled, "I know it's hard to believe, but handing over your body and soul to your Dom, especially when you're in a place that is new or unsettling, is the most liberating feeling in the world." Watching the grin spread across

Callie's face, Jace braced himself for what the little imp was going to say next.

"Oh sister, I can't tell you how great sub-space is when you go deep into a scene, but trust me, it's a ride you don't want to miss." Callie sighed and looked as if she was lost in a sweet memory for a few seconds before she blushed and seemed to come back to the present. "The bottom line is, you always have the club's safe word system to fall back on…if you start to get overwhelmed, say 'Yellow' and your Doms will stop and check in with you. I can't overemphasize how important that is, please don't hesitate to use it. And if things are just too much, call 'Red' and everything stops. And I do mean everything, not forever, but you're out of commission for twenty-four hours…club rules."

Holly leaned forward and gave Callie a warm hug, "Thank you so much. Damn it's great to have a friend again, it's been so long since I had anyone to really talk to I had almost forgotten how wonderful it can be."

Jace and Gage watched as the two women said their goodbyes, and it was only then that he realized Ian was standing behind him. The men that worked for Ian all swore he was better at sneaking up on people than they were and that was a hell of a compliment from a group of former Army Rangers and Navy SEALS. Ian simply smiled and said, "I think my *Carlin* deserves a reward, and I think it's time to bring out the little surprise I had made for her." Ian didn't elaborate and Jace didn't ask. But he knew Ian had been spending time in the island's small workshop recently, and that certainly opened up a world of possibilities.

Chapter 29

Walking into Club Isola's main room between her two husbands and having her senses bombarded with everything she heard and saw had been enough to take Holly's breath away. She tried to not let the sounds and sights overwhelm her, but once they crossed the threshold and she got her first look at the BDSM club's activities in full-swing, it was as if her feet had become rooted in place. The smell of leather and sex was thick in the air and the sounds of screams sent chills up her spine. There was so much to take in that her eyes felt like they weren't able to process enough information and suddenly she was all too aware of the way her other senses were scrambling to catch up and absorb the information as well.

The feel of the smooth stone floor under her bare feet felt cool and oddly comforting, like the touch of something solid and organic could keep her anchored somehow. The smell of sex soon divided into the scents of cleanliness, soap and the tangy citrus of shampoos and at the other end of the spectrum were the scents associated with human lust and release. The tangy musk of exposed genitals was heady and Holly felt her sex flood with moisture as she imagined the sweet scents her two Masters were going to add to that mix.

Listening to the crack of a whip followed by the soft gasps of the female sub tied to the St. Andrew's cross sent lightning bolts of electricity up her spine. Holly had watched Callie take several lashes the night of her wedding and collaring, but the marks Ian and Jace had left across her delicate back had been faintly pink. The marks across this sub's back were a deep red and the welts were already visible. Holly didn't realize she'd been backing up until she bumped into a solid wall of warm, hard muscle. "Stop sweetness, tell me what you see that has frightened you so." The comforting sound of Gage's voice in her ear was so overwhelming she sagged in relief. He whispered in her ear, "You have no idea how much I love the fact that your entire body relaxed at my touch and voice. Your body and soul recognize your Masters, baby, let them lead you tonight. You don't need that sharp mind of yours tonight—it will only make submitting more difficult and delay your pleasure."

He'd wrapped his arms around the filmy dress they'd given her to wear and as short as the damned thing was, his arms pressing under her unbound breasts was probably lifting the front enough that anyone looking was going to get a great view of her bare pussy. And while the idea should have mortified her, it didn't. In fact she felt another wave of moisture roll through her folds and wondered if it would soon be running in rivulets down her legs. "I…I was looking at those nasty looking welts on her back. And, well…I was remembering the faint pink lines that Master Ian and Master Jace left on Callie." Holly had glanced up to see Jace watching her intently, his expression devoid of anything but assessment.

"And you don't understand the difference? Is that it?" Gage hadn't stepped away from her and she was grateful that their conversation wouldn't be heard beyond the three of them. She was riveted to the scene in front of her and as the lashes continued to leave dark marks the sub's back Holly felt herself start to shake. She couldn't even answer because she felt like she was falling in a dark spiral. "Take a breath Holly—right now." Gage's voice had shifted and the command was unmistakable. She gasped in a breath and was relieved to see the darkness begin to fade.

Holly hadn't even realized that she'd dropped her gaze to the floor at the authoritative tone of Gage's voice, and when she raised her eyes Jace was standing directly in front of her. He was blocking her view of the scene and his eyes were filled with worry. "Pet, there are many people who enjoy pain. There are as many variations to BDSM as there are people. Our job as your Masters is to know your needs and your body even better than you do. We will always be watching even the smallest of your reactions. Lisa is being whipped by her Master as a reward. They have a long-term Ds relationship and he knows that she loves the endorphin release the pain gives her. She recently completed her pediatric residency and this is her reward for all of her hard work." He stepped to the side and her eyes went back to the scene, but this time she tried to focus on details other than the angry marks that were lined up in perfectly spaced precision diagonally across her slender back.

Gage spoke against her ear, "Listen to Lisa's moans. Those are the sounds of a woman fast approaching her climax. She is deep in sub-space, but she is so in tune with her Master that she won't come until he commands it. Lisa loves the pain and Master Brian loves her, so this is his gift to her even though he actually prefers other forms of play. Master Ian and Master Jace pulled their lashes with Callie because her loving husband didn't want her to have painful memories of their wedding night, but he also wanted to fulfill Club Isola's rules for a collaring ceremony. And baby, this is not something we expect from you. We already know that you respond well to small amounts of erotic pain, but you are not a pain slut. Trust us to know what you need, sweetheart. Thank you for your honesty. We want to hear if you have questions or concerns. While we won't always allow you to speak freely when we visit the club, tonight it's important that you don't hesitate to be open with one or both of us."

Holly felt Gage tighten his hold on her with one arm as he slid his other hand down until his fingers were trailing through her folds and the drag of his fingers told her that the arousal she'd felt earlier at the idea of being on display had disappeared as she'd watched the welts appearing on the woman's back in front of her. Drawing his dry fingers up in front of her, Gage chuckled, "See baby, this is pretty solid evidence that this is not what you need." Holly wasn't sure exactly why his words embarrassed her, but she felt her face go hot in an instant.

* * * *

Jace had watched Holly's reaction to the scene between Mark and Lisa, and he'd worried that she was going to go into a full-blown panic attack before Gage's voice had broken through the fear he'd seen in her eyes. They had known this scene was planned for tonight and had intentionally made it one of their stops while making their way to the smaller corner stage where they had planned their scene with Holly. While he hadn't enjoyed seeing the fear in her eyes, he was glad they'd made the time to double-check their mutual opinion that Holly wasn't ever going to respond positively to real pain. Despite all the competing smells in the room, Jace had known Holly was aroused earlier. And now he was sure her arousal was from Gage hiking her dress up enough to expose her to the room when he'd wrapped his arms around her, so it seemed their wife was a bit of an exhibitionist. *Interesting.*

Making their way to the smaller stage they turned the lights down so that the small box frame that Ian had built for Callie was the only thing visible. Jace watched as Holly's eyes went wide and her respiration became shallow. *Perfect.* When Gage had pulled a small rolling cart closer but left it so it was still just out of the light, they both stood with their arms crossed over their chests. "Strip" was all Jace said, but the command of his tone couldn't be missed.

When Holly started biting her lip and her eyes darted back and forth Jace wondered if they might end up having to punish her before they even started. He saw her eyes lock on something to her left and then she gave an almost imperceptible nod before pulling the straps of the dress over her slender shoulders and letting the soft silk slide to the floor. In his peripheral vision, Jace saw Callie standing just close enough that Holly would have recognized her. Ian's gorgeous wife had given her friend a thumbs up and then pointed to them as a reminder of where Holly's focus was supposed to be. Callie would be getting a nice large box of her favorite Donnelly's chocolates for her friendship and support of their sweet sub. Callie was a natural nurturer and Jace didn't doubt for a minute that she was going to be a terrific mother.

Gage secured Holly to the inside of the large wooden box that looked a lot like an empty picture frame. Ian had designed and built the unit for Callie because everything else in the club was designed for taller subs. Both Jace and Gage had been concerned about the strain on Holly's shoulders and the small scars from her recent close encounters of the violent kind with a hand gun. This scaled down version of one of their favorite apparatuses in the club was perfect. Jace glanced to the side and saw Ian quietly escorting Callie away from their scene. When he and Gage had spoken with Ian earlier this evening, his friend had assured him that he had planned a very special reward for his sweet wife. Her actions earlier today had warmed all three of their hearts.

But, Ian had also agreed with Jace's assessment that Callie's recent bratty behavior needed to be addressed and also agreed that he had probably been too lenient as a result of her pregnancy. He'd taken them into his playroom and shown them the spanking bench he and Mitch Grayson had designed and built. The thing had every bell and whistle imaginable. The padded leather could be warmed or cooled with the flick of a switch, various attachments would allow small hydraulic cylinders to automatically fuck the sub's ass or pussy with dildos of various sizes. The entire thing could be tilted until the sub was almost standing on her head and it rotated as well. But the best feature was that it had a removable panel over the belly area so that a pregnant sub could be restrained without any discomfort or danger to the new life cradled in her womb. Jace smiled to himself knowing that Callie was going to get some much needed attention tonight. He didn't doubt she was going to enjoy the hell out of Ian's latest toy.

Turning his full attention back to Holly, he moved into position in front of Holly. They had deliberately left enough space between them for a third person to step into her view, and Jace saw the slight crease in her brow, so he knew she had indeed noticed the fact they weren't shoulder to shoulder which was their norm. Jace spoke first, "Pet, do you remember the rules we outlined regarding who and when anyone besides one of your Masters sees your lovely naked body?"

Holly's eyes had been half-lidded with desire, but they were certainly wide open now. He fought down a chuckle and noticed Gage's lips twitch as well. "Y-yes, Sir." When he only raised an eyebrow at her, she quickly got the idea that he was expecting her to recount what they'd told her. "One of you has to be present if I am naked in anyone else's presence, except in emergency situations." He heard the trembling in her voice, oh yeah, she knew exactly what this was about.

Just before Jace responded, Dr. Don Whiteside stepped into the lighted circle. Gone were the surgical scrubs he'd been wearing the first time they'd met him. Those hospital standards had been replaced by skin-tight black leather pants, black boots, and a black silk shirt that was unbuttoned halfway down his tanned chest. Master Don assumed a stance similar to Jace and Gage's and just watched Holly intently. Jace heard her small gasp of breath when her gaze locked onto the doctor she'd seen just this afternoon. Jace fought his smile as he watched her entire body flush like a beautiful pink rose as she realized what was to come.

"Pet, did anything happen today at your appointment that you'd like to mention to your Masters?" He'd kept the steel in his tone, but he knew she was watching his face for any clue as to his real mood. Jace felt the corners of his mouth twitch and saw some of the tension drain from her lush body.

"I had to undress for my exam with Dr. Donnie Dark, but I kept on the ugly gown his nurse gave me and she stayed in the room at my request." Holly's eyes were wide with expectation and Jace was sure she'd deliberately baited him with her reference to the Dom standing between him and Gage by a nickname that was as disrespectful as it was funny. When he raised a brow at her she tried to act nonchalant, "Oh, sorry. Dr. Whiteside. I guess the nickname just seems to be so much more fitting…" Now he was certain she was playing and while he might have allowed it at home, he couldn't allow it in a scene at the club.

Stepping up close to her and grasping her chin he tilted her head back until she was forced to look directly into his eyes, "Pet, you had better amend that apology and do it quickly because that beautiful smart mouth of yours is just about to change the whole climate of the scene we have planned for you." He watched her breath catch and her eyes go wary. *That's better little sub. Don't go getting too big for the britches you aren't wearing.*

"I'm sorry, I know that was disrespectful. I'm nervous and bad stuff comes out of my mouth when I'm nervous. He has all that dark hair and commanding presence that is kind of like *Dark Shadows* meets Dr. House. Oh drat on a dead cat, I'm doing it again. But I really do apologize and I'll just stop talking now." Jace was biting the inside of his mouth to keep from laughing out loud at her description of Don White because it was so damned accurate and he was glad he was blocking her view of Don and Gage because he'd heard a snort of muffled laughter and wasn't sure which of them had been responsible.

"Very nice, pet. Now, I want to clear up something. Even if you are in an examination room, but you've only been given a thin little cotton gown, Master Gage or I need to be present. We aren't trying to be overbearing, we are trying to protect you. We have heard of subs and women in ménage relationships being accosted by the public, and being in any state of undress makes you particularly vulnerable. As you gain confidence and learn more about self-defense, we'll revisit this issue. But, my love, that is a long time in the future. And this applies to female doctors as well, pet." As he had pointed out their reasons for the rule, Jace had seen her eyes go glassy with unshed tears. Because Holly was a bright and creative woman, they would need to provide her with more information than some subs required, especially when it was related to anything she perceived as an infringement on the independence she'd worked so hard to earn.

When Jace stepped back again, Don had already moved back into the shadows and Jace was glad that it was just the three of them on the small stage. He wanted all of Holly's attention focused on her two Masters and the pleasure they were bringing to her body. She didn't realize it yet, but she *owned* both of her Doms. She held their hearts and souls in the palms of her dainty little hands.

Chapter 30

Five months later

Holly stared out the window of the waiting room watching the raindrops as they raced one another to the bottom of the floor to ceiling glass looking out over the lush strolling gardens of the private obstetrics clinic and birthing center. She had tuned out all of those around her, preferring to utter her prayers for her friend in private. Callie McGregor had gone into labor on her exact due date, but that seemed like it was the last thing that had gone right. They'd been waiting several hours and all they'd heard was that there had been some kind of "major event" as the nurse had referred to it and that Callie's entire medical team was working frantically to save both the mother and her precious baby girl.

Lost in thought, Holly smiled to herself as she remembered the fun she and Callie had shared over the past few months. They had become fast friends and had spent a lot of time together since Holly worked from home and Callie had cut back on her hours at the resort now that it was fully operational and in the hands of the top-notch management team Callie and Ian had selected.

Holly and Callie had enjoyed hitting garage sales despite the fact that neither they nor their husbands were financially strapped. They'd found a few bargains and Holly had loved watching Callie's eyes light up when she found something that was "just right and cheap, too." It was refreshing to see someone who hadn't forgotten what it was like to struggle and who also seemed so totally unaffected by her sudden wealth.

Looking up to see Ian step inside the room, Holly saw him call over her Aunt Daphne and Jace. They huddled for long moments and then Ian slipped back outside the room. Holly started to see black dots in front of her eyes and it was then that Gage's words broke through the fog, "Take a breath, sweetheart. Come on, you need to stay strong for your friend, don't panic until you hear what Ian had to say." She drew in a deep breath at his command and only then did she realize he knelt next to her chair and was holding her shaking hands in his. He was using his large, warm hands to massage her cold fingers. When she focused on his face, he smiled and kissed each of her palms before pulling her to her feet and walking her over to where Jace and Daphne were telling the others what Ian had shared.

Jace was speaking as they walked up, "As I said, Ian said they are cautiously optimistic that both Callie and their daughter will be fine. Evidently she had what the doctors called a major bleed and had they not already been here, they'd have most certainly lost both of them." He turned to Holly and smiled, "Ian said that in the brief moments that Callie was awake she was insistent that he accompany their daughter if she is transferred to a larger facility and she asked that you stay here with her. Ian has very reluctantly agreed to do that but as his friend I can tell you it is eating him alive, so let's hope that doesn't come to that."

Seeing the agony in Ian's expression had been almost enough to do Jace in, and now watching as Holly went stark white his heart clenched even tighter. Gage had his arm wrapped tightly around her waist and Jace saw him tighten it, so he knew Gage had noticed her reaction. "Pet, Ian felt like both his girls were on the mend now and they'll be transfusing her again as soon as they locate an AB negative donor because they didn't have enough on-site. Ian will fly a donor here if they can locate one."

Jace felt Holly's hand on his forearm, "I'm AB negative, let's go." Holly turned and walked out of the clinic's small waiting room, leaving Jace and Gage to scramble to keep up as she race-walked to the nurse's station.

Four hours later, they led their weak but very happy wife in to see her best friend. The two women hugged and after tearful thanks and congratulations, they made their way out the door with promises to visit again tomorrow after mama and baby Carly had gotten some much needed rest. Just as they all stepped into the hall Ian called out to them. Running to catch up before they reached the elevator, he pulled Holly into a tight hug. "I'll never forget what you did for my family, Holly. Anything that you ever need—if it's within my power to get it—it's yours. Don't hesitate to call me—ever."

Jace watched Holly look up at Ian and smile, "Ian, the only thing I'll ever ask of you is that you be the best husband and father you can be. I love Callie and I can't wait to get to know your beautiful daughter as well. Carly is gorgeous and I fully intend to the best faux-aunt ever." She smiled and hugged Ian again before pulling back. "Don't ever throw material goods at either of your ladies and think that it's good enough. Shower them with your love and affection, make sure they have a bit of your undivided attention each and every day. Those are the only things I'll ever ask of you." Holly hugged Ian one last time and then said, "Go. They need you."

Watching a single tear slide down Ian McGregor's cheek was a moment in time Jace knew he would never forget. After Ian turned to walk down the hall, he pivoted and pinned Jace and Gage both with a look that was pure Ian McGregor the Dominant and billionaire businessman, "Take very good care of her, she is a very important member of *my* family." He waited until they both nodded their understanding before turning once more to make his way back to Callie's room.

* * * *

Gage pulled Holly into his embrace and then turned slightly so that she was sandwiched between both he and Jace. "Damn, baby, you are un-fucking-believable. If I wasn't already totally in love with you, your words to Ian would have cinched it. I thought my heart would burst with pride knowing you are ours." He watched as her eyes softened and became shiny with her unshed tears. "I am humbled that you're my wife and that someday we'll be the ones walking back into your room after you've become the mother of our child. Hell, I hope there are several of those occasions." He leaned down and pressed a feathered kiss against the silky hair on the top of her head. "I love you with my entire heart, sweetheart. I just needed to remind you."

"I love you too, Gage…I love both you and Jace more than I can begin to tell you." She shifted just enough that she could see both he and Jace. Placing a soft, warm palm on each of their faces, her voice had gone bedroom soft. Gage had always marveled at how sweet Holly's voice was in their everyday interactions, but in the bedroom it became softer and deeper. The timbre of her words felt like sun warmed silk gliding over his skin and never ceased to enflame him. "You and Jace saved me, not just from that crazy preacher, but also from myself. You've opened the doors to my heart and let me know that all the longings I'd had weren't *wrong* just because they didn't meet the expectations of the other people in my life. There isn't any greater gift than enlightenment and acceptance."

Holly's green eyes were fast approaching the deep emerald they became when she was aroused letting Gage know it was time to get her someplace private before they were all naked and giving the clinic's staff and visitors something to talk about for the next twenty or thirty years. Gage couldn't remember a time in his life when he had felt more complete, standing here—knowing the woman who owned his heart was happy and fulfilled because of his love was just about as good as it got. Sharing her with a man he'd always considered one of his dearest friends—a man that he respected and trusted—was icing on the cake.

Gage watched as Jace smiled at Holly indulgently, "Pet, we need to get home. My need to fuck you is becoming almost more than I can control. We are only ten minutes from here and Ian will not hesitate to call us if he needs us." He leaned forward and brushed his lips teasingly over hers, "I need you, my love. I'll always need you. You complete me. But right now, I need you naked and under me, and if you don't want to do that in this hallway you need to step into that elevator." Gage was sure she hadn't even noticed the doors slide open or that he was holding them for her, but Jace's words had spurred her to action.

Just as they walked into their home Jace and Gage's phones both sounded with messages. Jace glanced at his first, and saw it was from Kalen so he decided to take a quick look. Since the man wasn't prone to chitchat the message was likely important.

Abby's primary tracker is off-line. Requesting permission to activate secondary. Will advise if we encounter a problem.

Jace quickly replied giving his team the go-ahead for the secondary tracker. Abby's job took her all over the globe and not everyone was thrilled with the headway his sister was making in her quest to find viable sources and applications for renewable energy. He and Ian had worked closely with Mitch Grayson to create three different trackers in order to ease their own minds that Abby was always safe, or at the very least they could always find her to check for themselves. Abby knew about the primary and secondary systems, but they hadn't shared the fail-safe system with her. Hell, she'd raised seven kinds of hell with him and Ian when they'd insisted on the first two systems.

Abby was absolutely brilliant, but she often became so engrossed in what she was working that her own safety took a backseat to whatever grindstone she had her nose pressed firmly against. She was also notorious for failing to replace the small batteries in the waterproof bracelet they'd given her. If the small batteries weren't changed every six months, the device would suddenly go off-line. It happened often enough that Jace had warned her about the little boy who cried wolf because he didn't want his team to get complacent about instituting the security protocol procedure they had established. Luckily it appeared Kaden was in the control center today so Jace was confident he'd have the issue resolved in short order. *Damn genius sister anyway, I swear the little imp knows when I'm about to sink my aching cock deep in my woman and she acts out just to annoy my ass. She ragged my ass about making her an aunt, and then she pulls this crap.*

When Jace looked up he saw the concern in Holly's eyes—it was time to erase that and replace it was arousal and longing. Even though they'd given Holly several swats at the club for failing to tell them about her appointment and for opening the door without checking who was on the other side, they'd kept things fairly light since it was her first public scene. She had responded well and Jace was looking forward to trying something more intense soon.

Moving so that he was close enough to press a soft kiss against her forehead, Jace said, "Don't worry about anything except how fast you can get naked and get upstairs, pet. Because your Masters intend to give you one swat for each second you are dressed after we are both naked, and love, we are damned fast when we're motivated." He waggled his eyebrows at her and smiled as he heard Gage's chuckle from behind him. When she didn't move, he grabbed the front of his own shirt and ripped it open sending buttons flying in all directions. He saw her eyes go as wide as saucers and heard her gasp of surprise, but then she turned and took off running toward the bedroom. He heard her shriek of laughter and saw she was shedding her clothes as she ran. She had literally left a trail of clothing all the way down the hall.

He turned toward Gage and smiled, "Well, that was pretty effective. Guess we'd better get a move on. Seems like a waste for our beautiful sub to be naked and alone."

Gage nodded, his soft laugh lightening his words, "She's so fucking perfect. I can't believe she's ours. Let's go make sure she's so happy and sated she never wants to be anywhere but between us— forever."

THE END

ABOUT THE AUTHOR

For years, I was accused of living in "Fantasy Land" so I decided to put it to use and started writing. I enjoy creating characters who are loveable but never perfect, who live in and visit all the places I'd love to go, and who overcome obstacles to find the sexy happily ever after I believe we all deserve. I fall in love with the characters I create and enjoy making them each wacky and wonderful in their own way.

The only consistent trait in my heroines is their inability to cook and that is the only trait they each have "inherited" from me. When I'm not working at my very ordinary job, I am either writing or reading. And even though my family professes to support my writing efforts, I'm fairly certain they are merely glad to see I've finally found an outlet for what they considered an over-the-top imagination.

For all titles by Avery Gale, please visit
www.bookstrand.com/avery-gale

Siren Publishing, Inc.
www.SirenPublishing.com

Lightning Source UK Ltd.
Milton Keynes UK
UKHW02f1454180418
321261UK00005B/331/P